ORPHAN TRAIN STRIKE

HEARTS ON THE RAILS 5

RACHEL WESSON

LONDONGATE PUBLISHING

Copyright © 2020 by Rachel Wesson

All rights reserved.

No part of this book may be reproduced in any form or by any electronic or mechanical means, including information storage and retrieval systems, without written permission from the author, except for the use of brief quotations in a book review.

CHAPTER 1

HOME FOR DESTITUTE GIRLS,
MANHATTAN, NEW YORK, NOVEMBER
1906

Alice hopped from one foot to the other wishing she had visited the convenience before the Matron called her name. Now she and the other children stood in line looking at Mrs. Twiddle, their visitor.

Alice gazed at her face, hoping to see her smile. She was frowning, her lips growing tighter by the minute as she kept glancing at the watch she carried. Was she late? Someone should tell her to leave, they would be fine in Matron's care. She was nice, well most times.

Alice couldn't wait any longer. She frantically pulled Matron's uniform and gestured toward the privy. Matron gave her a push out the door as if to hurry her up. Alice raced across the yard hoping to be back before Matron gave out the presents. Matron told them they would get a new dress and a surprise this afternoon.

When she came back, the children stood in line in front of Mrs. Twiddle. Alice took her new dress, a coat, knitted hat and gloves with glee. The brand-new bible she was less enthusiastic about. She hurried away with the other girls to try on their new clothes.

"Alice, you look beautiful. Your hair has even started to grow out."

Alice thanked Chloe with a smile. Chloe hadn't been in the Home for very long, only two months. She had come from another orphanage and was leaving soon to work.

"Shush, Chloe. You don't want Matron hearing you or she will shear her again or worse dip her head in Larkspur. She won't get new parents without hair, will she?"

Alice whirled around to face Dawn, one of the elder girls going on the trip. "I don't want new parents. I have parents."

Issy, a ten-year-old who'd been in the home since Alice could remember, put her hand on her hips. "Don't you start that again. You is the same as us. Orphans and you best get used to new parents.

Why do you think you got new clothes? You soft in the head."

Miss Baker, one of the house supervisors came in just in time to hear Issy's remark.

"Issy, stop that. Be kind." Miss Baker put her hand on Alice's shoulder turning her to face her. "Alice, we've been through this before. Your mother died so you have to go with the other girls on the train with Mrs. Twiddle. She will find you new parents who will give you a lovely house, you can go to school and have a wonderful life."

Alice couldn't see Miss Baker through her tears. "Can you come with us, Miss Baker?"

"No, Alice, I have to stay here ready for our new arrivals. You will be fine. Dawn and Chloe will look out for you younger girls and they won't let anyone behave badly." Miss Baker glared at Issy as she spoke. Issy remained stone faced.

Miss Baker bent down to Alice's level. "Alice, this is for you. You had it when you first came here just over two years ago. Matron put it away for you in case… well it doesn't matter why. Here take it." Miss Baker handed Alice a small cloth doll dressed in a bright blue dress with white flowers embroidered in the material. A letter A was embroidered in the corner of the doll's apron.

"Did my mother make this for me?" Alice asked, fingering the pieces of cloth used to make the doll's dress.

"I believe so, Alice. Someone who loved you. Now hurry and join the others. Mrs. Twiddle gets upset when anyone is late."

"Mrs. Twiddle looks like she is always upset," Issy said.

"Issy! Be nice. We have little in life, but kindness never cost anyone anything."

"Yes, Miss Baker." Issy threw over her shoulder as she left the smaller room.

"Alice, a moment. When you are all grown up, if you ever come back to New York, please come and say hello. I will probably still be here. Part of the furniture I am."

Alice couldn't breathe, the pain in her chest was too bad. She tried to move but her feet wouldn't obey her brain. She looked up and caught Miss Baker's tear-filled eyes. With a sob, she flung herself at the kind woman who had held her when she cried, looked after her when she fell ill with a high fever and nursed her back to health after measles gripped the orphanage. She couldn't remember a time when this woman wasn't by her side. "I love you, Miss Baker. I wish you were my mother."

Miss Baker held her close and Alice barely heard her whisper, "I do too." before she was pushed away. "Go now Alice and be good for Mrs. Twiddle. She means well. Just remember that in the days ahead. Chloe and Dawn have both promised to keep an eye on you."

Alice didn't care, not anymore. She didn't want to leave New York and everyone and everything she knew. She held tight to the doll Miss Baker had given her, deciding to call her Agatha. She didn't know why but she liked that name.

She joined the back of the queue of children now making their way out of the orphanage and down the street. She waved goodbye to the Matron and the other children. She walked past boxes of food piled up on the steps of the orphanage, spotting figs, dates, bananas and some oranges. Were they coming on the trip too? She loved oranges.

CHAPTER 2

*L*arge snowflakes fell from the New York sky coating everything in white like a blanket. Alice stepped on board the horse-drawn streetcar wondering how the snow made even the dirtiest things look wonderful. Would her friends be out throwing snowballs? Sometimes, Miss Baker played with them. If she was caught, Matron told Miss Baker she was nothing but a child herself, but Matron would smile when she said this. Miss Baker had grown up in an orphanage Matron had worked at previously and came with Matron when she moved to the Home for Destitute girls. Someone said, it had improved a lot since Matron joined. Alice couldn't remember a time when Matron wasn't in charge.

An automobile horn made her jump. Judging by the noise the horses made they didn't like these new inventions either. Alice gripped her doll. Maybe Mrs. Twiddle would change her mind. Would the snow fall heavily enough to send them back to the home?

It didn't appear so. The streetcar kept moving away from the home in the direction of the river. Chloe said they would take a ferryboat across to New Jersey. Alice didn't like the water. She had nightmares about it, but Matron said she was being silly. Alice's heart beat faster as they got nearer the river. She sniffed at the smells of the dock area, images filling her mind. A large boat, lots of women and children. A sunny day, people laughing, carrying picnic baskets. She shook her head trying to clear the pictures from her mind.

Dawn, the English girl from the orphanage glanced at her. "Alice, what's wrong? You're as pale as a sheet." Dawn looked under her lashes at Mrs. Twiddle who had told them to sit in silence.

Alice loved the older girl who'd been so kind to her since she'd arrived in the orphanage. Dawn had come to America with her older brother but they'd got separated. Like Alice, she had no family. "I'm scared, Dawn. I hate the river."

Dawn held her hand tight. "I will be with you. The ferry is safe, just like taking a train but it's on the water. It will be exciting."

Alice held onto Dawn's hand, but she didn't feel excited. She felt sick. This place gave her a funny feeling in her belly.

"Alice, cheer up. It won't take long and it's the only way to get to Erie railroad." Dawn held her hand so tight she left a mark, but Alice didn't tell her off. She trusted Dawn, the older girl looked after her and made sure the others didn't tease her.

Chloe made funny faces, but Alice couldn't laugh. She stared at the water as she cuddled as close to Dawn as she could get.

"It won't take long, I promise." Chloe whispered as Mrs. Twiddle gave them a dirty look. "The train will be waiting for us on the other side of the water."

"Mrs. Twiddle, how long will the train take to go to Illinois?"

"Stop talking. You ask too many questions. We will get there when we arrive and no sooner." Mrs. Twiddle glared at Issy but Issy just turned her face to the water. Nothing seemed to upset Issy. Alice hoped she would be more like the other girl when she was ten years old.

Once aboard the ferry, Alice watched the Manhattan skyline disappear from view. She felt Issy's hand in hers, the other girl squeezing. "That's the last time we will see home isn't it Alice?"

Shocked Issy was crying, Alice felt real fear for the first time. Issy wasn't afraid of anything, not spiders or snakes or the horrible punishments some of their teachers dished out. She'd never seen her cry.

"You will come back when you are bigger, you'll see Issy. You can tell Matron exactly what you think of her breakfast, in person." Dawn tickled the young girl making Issy giggle. Then Issy pulled Alice's hair.

"What did you do that for?" Alice complained.

"Dunno. Guess I don't want you thinking I've gone soft." With that Issy left, heading toward some other hapless victim on the other side of the ferry. Alice didn't really mind, Issy hadn't hurt her not really. And in a funny way, it made her feel better the other girl worried too.

As the ferry moved into the middle of the river, Alice started to shake. Dawn tightened her hold on her hand. "Alice, don't be afraid. I know you are only six, but you will have a better life out of New York. I know it."

Alice couldn't think of being anywhere else. Her gaze focused on the water. Shivers ran through her body making her teeth rattle. She tried clamping them together, but it was no use. She stifled a scream. Closing her eyes, she could feel the cold water flowing over her but there was heat too. Flames, a boat in flames. Her fingers reached to the scar on the back of her head.

"Alice, Alice stop it. You'll hurt your head. What is it?"

"The water, I want to get off, I have to get off." Alice rose but Dawn dragged her back to her seat.

"Stop it. You can't get off in the middle of the river. You're scaring me. We are almost on the other side." Dawn rarely spoke so sharply. Alice looked up but Dawn didn't look angry, she looked terrified.

"Dawn, the water, it scares me. When I close my eyes, I see lots of flames on the water."

Dawn laughed and hugged Alice closer. "Now I know you have nothing to worry about. Who ever heard of water going up in flames? You daft ha'-porth." Dawn's English accent only came through rarely. Alice knew she wouldn't convince her friend it had happened. The river had been on fire but when or where she didn't know. She moved closer

"What did the palace look like, Dawn? Was it huge with fancy carpets like Matron's office?"

"Nah Alice it was much nicer than Matron's office. They make the palace doors of pure gold. And the carpets, your feet sink right into them. The palace is so big it would be hard for it to fit in New York."

Mrs. Twiddle overhead this last bit. "Please stop telling silly lies, Dawn. Alice, Dawn has never stepped inside the palace. Bigger than New York with gold doors. Whatever next?"

Alice said nothing. She knew Dawn added details to the story, the last time she'd told it she'd said they made the doors of the best wood you could find in the whole of England. Alice didn't care. She knew Dawn was trying to get her mind off the water and it had worked. Sort of. For now, they were on the other side.

"Thanks Dawn. Your story helped."

Dawn smiled but her eyes still looked sad. Alice wished Dawn still had her brother, she seemed to really miss him.

CHAPTER 3

ITALIAN QUARTER, NEW YORK,
NOVEMBER 1906

"Maria, hurry. You will make me late and that costs me money. I hope Mr. Reinhart asks someone else to teach you the job. Mama can't afford for me to lose wages."

Maria pulled on her dress, only half listening to her sister. Rosa was always moaning about something or other. She ran a brush through her hair before pinning it up out of her way. Standing up she pushed her feet into her shoes, trying to calm the butterflies in her stomach.

"Maria Mezza, did you hear me?"

Rosa's strident tones grew louder before she heard the door opening.

"The whole tenement heard you. There's nothing wrong with my ears. I'm coming." Maria grabbed her lunch from the table, gave her mama a quick kiss and ran out the door after her sister. She held her nose as she walked down the steps to the outside street. The smell was never good in the tenements although it wasn't as bad as it had been in the summer. Heat and overcrowded buildings didn't mix well. For a second she closed her eyes, daydreaming of her childhood. Days spent working alongside her parents, picking lemons, olives and other fruits before racing her cousins to the sea for a swim, enjoying the feel of the warm sun on her skin. Her imagination wasn't good enough to keep the memory of the sun alive, given the cold morning temperature of her current home. Shivering, she hurried to catch up with Rosa.

"How many shirtwaists do you make in a day?" Maria asked trying to find some common ground with her sister.

"Grignolla! It takes up to ten different people to make one shirtwaist. Some girls sew the sleeve seams, others sew the cuffs and collars. I work on the machines, but you will be a learner. That means your job will be to cut the loose threads off the ends of the finished shirtwaists."

"Rosa Mezza, don't you call me a greenhorn. It might be my first day at your factory but who left

ORPHAN TRAIN STRIKE

school last week. I can read English and do math. I don't want to be a seamstress for the rest of my life."

Rosa just threw her a dirty look before smiling sweetly at various tradesmen who were opening their stalls. "Buon Giorno, Buon Giorno," the traders called out good morning as they set out their goods. Maria loved the run up to Christmas and looked with interest at the items for sale. She had knitted some mittens for Mama and Rosa and a scarf for Papa, but she thought he might prefer some roasted chestnuts instead. Her stomach growled at the smell. She didn't notice Rosa had walked so far ahead until her sister roared her name.

"Maria!"

Walking so fast, Maria didn't see the puddle. The cold water seeped into her shoe making her knitted sock stick to her foot. Yuck. She slipped off the shoe and tried to rub her foot, but it only made things worse. The shoes she was wearing, Rosa's castoffs, had a hole in the sole but there was no money to replace them. Not with papa out of work again.

Poor papa, sitting at the kitchen table surrounded by women. When mama suggested her husband help with making the artificial flowers,

Maria held her breath waiting for her father to explode. Instead, he sighed and pulled up a chair. His large hands with their stained and broken fingernails overshadowing the small pieces of flowers her mother was making. Mama could make sixty cents a day, but papa was lucky if he made fifteen to twenty.

She knew why he did it. They needed the four dollars for the weekly rent. The rent collector wasn't going to accept any excuses, and they had nobody in America to lend them money. Back home in Sicily, things had been different. Everyone had been poor, that was true, but they had helped each other out more. Or so it seemed listening to the older people talking of the old country. She didn't remember being poor. They had grown most of their own food. Papa had gone fishing with his brothers to supplement the produce from their small farm holding. It was so different back in Sicily to the streets of New York. Here, you could barely see the sky with all the surrounding buildings. Papa said they would go to the seaside in America one day. But now that he was injured, that day might take longer to arrive.

"Maria, hurry. You can't daydream like that in the factory. You won't last a day. Mr. Reinhart is only taking you on as a favor to me. He knows I am one of his best workers."

Maria poked out her tongue at her sister's back but said nothing. Rosa slapped like their mama, it stung for hours. She moved quicker until she was walking abreast of her sister.

"Rosa, do you think papa will go back to work soon?" Maria knew her papa missed his job on the building works. He loved being outdoors although sometimes he would reminisce preferring the weather back home. He hated being cooped up indoors, but it was more than that. His pride was hurting having to do women's work and living off his wife and daughters.

Rosa rolled her eyes. "What are you asking me for? I don't know. His shoulder is hurt bad. You saw him when he came home. He almost cried when Mama took off his jacket."

Sorry she had mentioned it, Maria remained silent for the rest of their walk. Her stomach grumbled. She patted her jacket pocket, checking her sandwich was still there. Tempted to eat it, she resisted knowing she would starve at lunchtime.

Rosa pulled her out of the way as somebody ditched their dirty water from their window. "Careful sister, we're not in Sicily now."

Grateful not to be wet, Maria flashed her sister a smile. Rosa wasn't so bad. She worried about Mama and the family and money. She should think about her own life as she was at the age when most Italian girls got engaged if not married. Maria scowled thinking of Rosa's boyfriend. Paulo Greco was Cosa Nostra, and Papa always said his family didn't marry into the mafia. Her papa rarely flew into rages, he was a peaceful man until he read about protection rackets or people being beaten up or worse murdered. Mama often told her husband to shush as talking against some families was akin to asking for trouble. Rosa didn't seem to care. She liked the attention, people knew Paulo Greco. Rosa said he had a distinguished future ahead of him. Sometimes Rosa could be stupid. Paulo would be lucky to live to be twenty, given his gangster lifestyle. Maria sighed but didn't respond to the quizzical look from her sister. Rosa wouldn't take any notice of her opinion.

Her sister didn't see her as anything but an annoying hindrance. Maybe that would change when they were both working together in the same place.

"Maria, you will share my locker. It costs 25

cents a week to keep our hats and coats locked up. Don't sign up for another one."

Maria nodded.

"You have your scissors?"

"Yes, Rosa, they are still in my pocket!" Maria snapped. How many times would Rosa ask her the same question?

"Don't snap at me. I have to pay 5 cents for every needle I use. Mama needs every cent we earn, so you have to be careful."

Maria realized Rosa was even more worried about their parents and their financial problems than she'd realized. Overwhelmed with guilt, Maria spoke softly. "Yes, Rosa."

All too soon, they arrived at a metal door. Standing like a guard, was a portly older gentleman wearing his glasses on the end of his nose. He had a gold watch in his hand and kept glancing at it. He frowned as Rosa introduced her.

"Mr. Reinhart, this is Maria my fifteen-year-old younger sister. Her hands are clean and she is a quick learner."

Maria held her hands out to the boss, but he seemed more interested in what she was wearing. Shivers went up her arms at the look in his eye. Her brother had a similar look when he was staring in the store window at the candy display.

"You will start with Madame Stein. She can work and teach you at the same time. Take care not to damage anything. You do, you pay."

She jumped as Rosa kicked her shin, motioning with her head. She forced a smile. "Thank you, sir. I will be careful."

He had moved onto someone else. Maria followed Rosa up some rickety wooden steps losing count as they kept climbing.

"The lift is out of action, again!" Rosa panted but Maria was breathing too heavily to answer back. Finally, they arrived at the sixth floor. Maria resisted the urge to hold her nose, not sure whether the smell was worse than the dust which made her want to sneeze. The air was stagnant, the windows on one side of the floor were closed, their grimy appearance blocking out most of the light. Remnants of cloth, thread and lint dusted every surface and covered the floor. The light from the gaslights gave everyone in the room a ghostly like appearance.

Rosa showed Maria where the restroom was and her locker to store her coat before returning to the room with the rows of sewing machines.

"Pay attention to Mrs. Stein, she's been here forever. She knows what the bosses expect."

Maria resisted the urge to slip her hand into her sisters. She took slow breaths trying not to inhale the dust while also calming her nerves. There were so many girls and women in the room, she couldn't tell how many.

Rosa took her seat at her sewing table after pointing out Mrs. Stein, a wizened old lady with few teeth sitting at the far end of the room. Maria made her way around the gaggle of women sitting behind the row of sewing machines.

"Mrs. Stein? I am Maria, Rosa's sister. Mr. Reinhart told me to sit with you."

"Sit there. Hope you're a fast learner. We have a mountain of work."

At her words, the machines sprung to life with the wooden floorboards vibrating as the women fed the cloth under the needles. Stunned, Maria watched in awe as a lady fed the cloth around the needle flashing up and down, sure the woman would sew her fingers.

"Maria, pay attention."

Maria took the stool and watched as Mrs. Stein showed her how to snip off the loose threads from the material. She couldn't believe the number of shirtwaists sitting on the table. They couldn't finish all of them today, could they?

"Maria, you listening? You can't mark any of the white shirtwaists as they would deduct the cost from your earnings. Work as quickly as you can but don't cut the shirtwaist itself. Any chance they get, they will mark you down. You hear?"

Maria nodded.

Mrs. Stein smelled funny, like the pickles they sold on the market. She wasn't as old as she'd initially thought either but her humped back and way of peering at her work reminded Maria of her grandmother. The old woman had stayed behind in Messina, bedridden with no teeth. But she'd had kind eyes and always had a treat for Maria when she came to visit. Usually some figs or other sweet fruit. Tears filled her eyes as she remembered being pulled from her grandmother's arms on the day they emigrated to America, but she brushed them away impatiently. Rosa sent her a curious look but went back to her work.

After less than half an hour, Maria's back ached, and she needed to stretch her legs but nobody else moved. No one talked either although the room wasn't silent the whirling of the machines made an awful racket. Snip, snip. Her fingers grew red with the pressure of the scissors. She couldn't do this day in day out. She'd go mad. She glanced at Mrs. Stein who was sewing seams. That didn't look much better but at least her fingers wouldn't be getting blisters. She shifted in her seat, she needed to relieve herself and holding it was causing her discomfort. Mrs. Stein looked up, her eyes flashing with anger.

"What's wrong with you girl, you've slowed down. It's quicker you should get."

"I need the..." Maria fumbled for the correct word for toilet, "Lavatory."

Mrs. Stein mumbled something Maria couldn't hear before she returned her attention to her work. Maria half rose from her seat.

"Wait. Reinhart will dock your wages if you take a break now."

Maria couldn't wait. Didn't the woman know what it was like when you had to go.

"Wait? But how long?" Maria pushed her knees together.

"It's lunchtime in three hours."

Three hours? Her face grew hot as she looked around before leaning closer to Mrs. Stein.

"I can't wait that long, I'll have an accident. Please, Mrs. Stein. I really need to go."

Mrs. Stein looked around, causing Maria to do the same. There was no sign of Reinhart. "Go but be quick. Don't make a habit of it either."

"Yes, Mrs. Stein." She ran before her prophecy came true.

CHAPTER 4

The hours dragged by, she kept checking the clock to see if it was working. She got faster but Mrs. Stein still grunted with disapproval. All around her the women worked without chatting. She didn't know how they kept going. She caught Rosa glancing at her twice, but her sister's expression was hard to read. Rosa had said they would finish by six, but that time came and still they worked. Maria looked at the clock so often she was sure the hand wasn't moving. The seconds seemed to be minutes. Half past six, quarter to seven, seven. When would it end?

Her back and fingers ached, and her eyes were closing. She forced them to stay open terrified she would let the scissors slip and damage the shirtwaist. She didn't know how much one of them cost but Rosa had warned her earlier it was more than they would pay her for a week. Then silence fell. It took a couple of seconds for her to realize the machines had stopped moving. The women stretched and stood chatting to their neighbors or rushing to get their things. Maria sat where she was, too tired to move.

"Come on, Maria. Time to go home."

She looked up at her sister's voice, blinking back tears. Rosa put a hand on her shoulder. "Mama's waiting for us at home." Rosa squeezed her shoulder and this gesture of support was enough to get Maria moving.

Mrs. Stein stood up, smiling. "You did well today Maria. See you tomorrow."

"Thank you, Mrs. Stein for being so patient."

Maria followed Rosa out of the building, listening to the surrounding chatter. Some were speaking English, she recognized the language from school. Most spoke Italian with some speaking what she thought was Yiddish. She didn't have any Jewish friends, but she enjoyed going to the Jewish market sometimes.

She could barely speak to Rosa as they made their way home. Every muscle in her body ached, her shoulders felt like they would never straighten again and she couldn't wait for her bed. She was hungry but too tired to eat.

"It will get easier, little sister." Rosa put her arms around her shoulder as Maria stumbled on something in the dark. Maria was glad of her sister's help, but she didn't speak. That took energy she didn't have.

Once home, everyone wanted to know how she had got on. She tried to keep her eyes open at dinner but failed miserably. Mama shooed her off to bed giving her a cuddle as she tucked her in. Maria couldn't remember the last time, Mama had put her to bed.

Mama whispered, telling her how proud she was of her. "Maria, I know you wanted to be something more. To be a teacher or something. Papa and I wish it could be different. We had such dreams coming to America." Her mother sighed. "Maybe in time…"

Maria sat up despite wanting to sleep. "Mama, tomorrow will be better. Please don't worry. I love you."

"I love you too. Now sleep little one."

Maria didn't need telling twice.

CHAPTER 5

The next day wasn't any easier it was harder. Mrs. Stein tried her best to help her, but Reinhardt acted as if Maria should know enough to work on her own. He put a mound of shirtwaists in front of her telling her everyone would have to stay back if she failed to get them done. She snipped the threads as fast as she could, the finished mound slowly increasing but it didn't seem to impact the size of the unfinished mound.

She went as fast as she could but was terrified of making a mistake. As the clock struck five, she knew there was no chance of her finishing the work they had given her. The surrounding ladies muttered about having to work late. Mrs. Stein surprised her by taking some of her work and even

Rosa stepped in, taking a load of shirtwaists from Maria and finishing them in no time.

"You can pay me back one day, Maria." Rosa flashed her a smile. She was lucky to have a wonderful family and so what if she didn't become a teacher? Some things were more important.

* * *

THE DAYS ROLLED into each other with no variety. The blisters on her fingers hardened as she got faster. She caught the supervisor trying to put more shirtwaists on her unfinished pile. She stared at him but couldn't say a word. He had the control and the look on his face told her he knew it. But again Mrs. Stein came to her rescue.

"Mr. Reinhard, I will divide out those extra shirtwaists between us. Maria has too many and I worry she will get careless."

Maria sucked in her breath, not daring to look up. Would he fire her or Mrs. Stein or both of them. But Mrs. Stein hadn't finished.

"She is a good worker, one of the best I've trained but she won't be any use to us if she gets fired."

Maria waited for the supervisor to reply. His

breath made her stomach retch but she pretended not to notice him moving closer. He was almost touching her shoulder. She couldn't move now even if she wanted to, the fear paralyzed her.

"You might have a point Mrs. Stein. Careful girl, our factory has a good reputation for our product."

He moved away but it took Maria a few seconds to move. She glanced at the older woman, the expression of loathing in Mrs. Stein's eyes directed toward the boss's back made her shudder. Mrs. Stein muttered something but Maria couldn't understand her. The older woman must have sensed her gaze.

"Thank you, Mrs. Stein. You saved me."

"I meant it. You're a hard worker. Now what are you staring at me for? That won't get them done will it?" Mrs. Stein pointed her finger at the pile of work. Maria snatched the next shirtwaist and worked even harder. That evening she told Rosa what had happened.

"He won't like it. Mrs. Stein should be more careful."

Stung Maria retorted. "I thought you'd be happy she helped me."

Rosa shrugged. "Today she helped, tomorrow or

the next day he will try the same trick. That's the way things are."

Sunday was their only day off. Mama insisted the whole family dress in their best clothes, the girls with their hair covered and walk to Church together. Maria saw Rosa's face flush as she spotted Paulo. Mama must have seen him as she looked directly in his direction yet Mama didn't raise a hand or even smile in acknowledgement. Instead, she ushered her family into their normal pew but instead of Rosa sitting on the edge, Maria's sister found herself between her Papa and older brother, Benito. Maria hid a smile. Her mama didn't miss much.

"Maria, put your head down and pray for your sins. Hold your sister's hand. Louisa, how many times do I have to tell you to sit still in his Lord's house? Sophia Mezza, do I have to tell Papa you are whining?" Mama whipped her family into shape only lapsing into silence when the smell of incense announced the priest.

Maria let the Latin words flow over the top of her head. There was only one thing she prayed for and that was a return to Sicily, back to Messina and her grandmother. If they went home, her parents would smile again. Papa would look like the young man he was and not like a grandfather. Mama would stop crying at night when she thought nobody could hear her. If we cannot go home, Dear Lord, please move us to the countryside in America. Somewhere my parents would be happy where Papa could recover his strength. Please God, please.

Maria didn't know where to find the countryside. Her teacher at school had told her about California where lemons grew and grapes and other fruits. The temperature was warmer and people could swim on the beaches. That sounded like a good place to live. She'd forgotten about it until Mrs. Stein mentioned her sister's cousin who lived on the West Coast.

Maybe she should mention it to Papa. Give him hope of a better life. A sharp pinch from Mama brought Maria back to reality as the Priest invited his parishioners to come to communion.

Louisa fidgeted beside her.

"Sit still Louisa, you heard mama. She will be furious if you cause people to stare at us."

"Yes Maria." Louisa replied.

Maria couldn't help smiling. She loved her younger sisters but Louisa was her favorite. She reminded Maria of her younger self, always running never walking. But Louisa hadn't experienced the freedom of Messina, the space and the walks along

"Sorry Alice, I didn't mean to let go but someone pushed me. You are fine now, stop shaking. I won't lose you again, I promise."

Alice didn't answer, she couldn't. She was shaking so much, her teeth chattered in her head.

Finally, they reached their train and were the first ones to board the car. Mrs. Twiddle told them where to sit and everyone did as they were told even Issy.

"We will change at Chicago, Illinois which is some miles away so for now make yourself comfortable. I don't want to hear anyone complaining. You girls should consider yourselves lucky. There are plenty of more deserving children who could have new homes. Well-behaved young girls."

Alice moved backward and forward on the horsehair-covered benches. They were dreadfully uncomfortable; the horsehair made her itch and the hard seat made her butt hurt. But she dare not complain. Dawn dished out sandwiches while Chloe rationed the water. Mrs. Twiddle warned them not to go near the trains water supply no matter how thirsty siting in the smoke-filled car made them. It was dangerous.

It was cold despite a small coal-burning furnace in the carriage's corner. The children took their turns sitting near it, but this was double edged sword. Yes, you got slightly warmer, but you also got more of the dirt and dusts spewed out by the heater. It was impossible to keep their new woolen dresses clean. Looking out the widow they spotted men in the fields.

Dawn poked her gently. "Look Alice, the farmers are using bobsleds. I heard they are great fun if you use them to go down a hill. Would you like to try it? Maybe at your new home?"

"I don't want a new home. I want to go back to Miss Baker." Alice refused to look out the window. Would it be cold in Chicago or wherever they were going?

When the train stopped, they could get off to stretch their legs with a brief walk. It was nice to have time to run and get away from the horsehair material. Alice stuck to Dawn, clinging to her arm even when the older girl got fed up. She wasn't letting the last friendly face she knew disappear.

CHAPTER 7

The train sped through the countryside. Darkness and light, field after field with the odd house thrown in to break up the monotony. Alice couldn't remember ever being so bored. Even Dawn's best attempts to cheer them all up failed miserably.

Finally, they arrived in Chicago, Illinois. The people spoke funny compared to the New Yorkers they had left behind. They got a horse-drawn omnibus to the Chicago Milwaukee and St Paul's train station.

"Are we staying in a hotel Mrs. Twiddle? Matron used to tell us stories about Harvey hotels where the women worked in the West."

"Isabella, you ask too many questions. Who

Issy whispered, "They wanted to say goodbye to you, but Mrs. Twiddle said they couldn't. Said you would be too upset. I saw Dawn crying. I swear I did. Even that Chloe had tears in her eyes. I'm sorry Alice, they went when Mrs. Twiddle took you to the privy. I think she planned it like that."

Alice hated Mrs. Twiddle. It was her fault they were here so far away from Miss Baker and now Dawn and Chloe. She wished the woman would disappear.

But her wish didn't come true. Mrs. Twiddle sat opposite them for the whole trip meaning they spent most of it sitting in silence.

The train pulled up at the next station. Alice wiped the sleep from her eyes, squinting out the dirt-covered windows. Was this it? Were her new parents waiting on the platform? She pushed her hair back from her face, licking her fingers to flatten it into place. She rubbed her hands down her dress. It had been new and clean when they left New York but that had been almost a week ago.

Sitting up, she wished Dawn and Chloe were still on the train. Her friends from the orphanage would have held her hands and told her everything would be fine. Why couldn't they have taken her

The couple walked off leaving Alice to follow them. They hadn't even introduced themselves. What did they want her to call them? Maybe they were shy?

As they walked toward a parked wagon, Alice heard the train whistle. She glanced behind her as the train and her last remaining friend disappeared.

CHAPTER 8

The man helped his wife into the front seat of the wagon. He picked Alice up and deposited her in the back among the goods they'd bought in town. Alice hung onto the sides as the man whipped the horse and they were off. She watched her surroundings with interest. It didn't seem like a big town. There was a main street with a grocery store, a blacksmith and livery stable. She thought the small building next to the church might be a schoolhouse.

As Mr. Ackerman drove the wagon away from town, Alice noted the buildings grew sparser. She saw what looked like houses in the distance but none on the main road. After about fifteen minutes, they turned off the main road and onto a track towards a house sitting in the middle of a large field. The brick house was bigger than she'd expected with two stories, the top one having a white-fenced balcony and lots of windows. Were her new family rich? Chickens squawked as they scattered out of the way of the wagon.

To the left of the house stood a barn. She saw a vegetable patch to the right. There were sounds of an animal howling as if in pain but the couple didn't comment. Alice clenched her hands, she didn't think they would like it if she held them over her ears to stop the noise.

Mr. Ackerman jerked the horse to a stop and pushed the brake into place. Then he jumped down. He helped his wife before turning to Alice.

"What are you waiting for? Jump."

Alice looked over the edge of the wagon. It was rather high. She glanced at his face. He stared back at her making her stomach clench. She moved to the edge but before she could jump, he pulled her. She half fell to her feet, bruising her knee on the wheel.

"Do as you're told, girl." He roared before turning on his heel and marching toward the front door. Alice didn't know whether she should wait or follow him. She glanced at Mrs. Ackerman, but the woman didn't appear to notice her. She walked off in the house's direction. Alice tried to reach for her basket as Agatha was inside, but the wagon was too high. She strolled into the house following in the couple's footsteps.

The house was very dark despite the number of windows. Clenching her hands, she drifted toward the sound of voices.

"This is the kitchen. You will help Eliza with her chores."

"Yes, Sir."

"You will call Eliza, Mother. I will be Father."

"Yes, si...Father." Alice stumbled over the words, watching his face. The lines at the side of his mouth became more defined. Terrified, she couldn't look at his eyes. Why was he angry?

"Ned, leave her be. I got to get the food on the table. See to Molly will you."

Alice's hopes rose. *Molly.* There was another girl in the house. Maybe they could be friends. She missed Dawn and Chloe, even Issy.

"Milking Molly is women's work. Can't she do it?"

Alice stared back at him. Molly was a cow? She'd never been near a cow. She'd seen them in fields and knew that was where you got milk from but that was the extent of her knowledge.

"Ned, this once won't hurt ya. Go on, the noise is giving me a headache. I didn't have time to milk her this morning before we left for the train." Eliza glared at Alice who shrank back. "Leave me and her to find our feet."

Ned went, muttering the whole time. Alice glanced at the woman she should call Mother.

"Don't stand there gawking at me. Set the table or don't you know how?"

Alice put her coat on a chair and looked around her. Mrs. Ackerman pulled out some knives and forks, three plates and three cups and set them on the side of the table. "Set three places, proper like. We have nice table manners in this house."

Alice did as they asked. She smiled once she'd finished but Mrs. Ackerman ignored her.

A mouthwatering smell filled the kitchen. Alice hoped her stomach wouldn't grumble. She couldn't remember the last time she'd eaten a hot meal. They'd only had rolls on the train.

"Fill the jug with water from the sink. Then sit down. I'm nearly ready."

Alice took a seat and waited. The door opened admitting Ned who glared at her but didn't comment. He had her basket in one hand but instead of giving it to her, he let it fall on the floor near the back door. He dumped the milk pail on the table causing some milk to slop out over the sides. He didn't seem to notice and Eliza said nothing but Alice noted her new mother's lips thinned.

He took the seat opposite to her. Mrs. Ackerman placed a plate covered in a mound of stew in front of her husband. She dished out a smaller portion for herself and only then did she put two spoonsful of food on a plate for Alice. She gave her one portion of corn bread before dividing the rest between herself and her husband.

Alice picked up the bread only to jump as he rapped her knuckles with his knife.

"Don't you dare start eating before we say Grace."

Alice mumbled an apology as she blinked back the tears. Her hunger had driven all thoughts of prayers from her mind. She waited for him to say a long grace, listening as he asked for forgiveness and understanding for the lost sheep who'd joined the household. She hadn't seen any sheep outside but now wasn't the time to ask questions.

As soon as his meal was over, he disappeared. Alice was glad, she thought of the two, Eliza might be easier to get on with. She jumped up and started clearing the dishes.

"The hot water is on the stove. Make sure you don't break anything. Call me when you've finished."

Alice couldn't quite reach the sink. Seeing her struggle, her new mother dragged a chair over.

"I'll help you today as it's your first day, but you do it starting tomorrow."

Alice nodded. She'd agree to anything to get a smile, but the woman's facial expression never changed. For a second, Alice closed her eyes and focused on a picture of Miss Baker.

"Can't see nothing with your eyes closed, girl."

"Yes ma'am, I mean Mother."

Eliza didn't react. She threw the dishes into the hot water, the splashes burning Alice's hands and face. Her dress protected the rest of her body. She moved away quickly as the next lot of dishes hit the water. In no time, her new mother had them washed. Alice dried and placed each plate and the cutlery carefully on the table. They worked in silence, not a comfortable one. Alice repeated a prayer over and over hoping someone would listen and make this be part of a bad dream. She would wake up and find herself in a nice house.

"You finished yet?"

Alice glanced up as she placed the last plate on the table.

"Yes, ma..mother."

"Grab your things and I will show you where you sleep. Do you have a nightgown?"

Alice nodded. She followed the woman up the wooden stairs.

"Your room is this one." Eliza pushed open a door to a small room with a bed and a desk. On the desk was a jug and water bowl. The bed had a rough-looking blanket on it, but it was her own room. Alice stared. Eliza tutted.

"What do you say, girl?"

"All this is for me? Just me?"

"Don't see anyone else, here do you?"

"Thank you Mother. I never had a room of my own before." Impulsively Alice stepped forward to give the woman a hug, but the woman withdrew so quickly, Alice nearly spun off her feet.

"You keep it clean and tidy, you hear?"

"Yes Mother." Alice tried to keep her voice steady, but the tears made it difficult.

"Bed now. We get up early around here."

Her mother closed the door, leaving Alice alone. She glanced around the walls of the room before she made her way fully dressed to the bed. She took

***

"Good morning, Mother."

Eliza didn't react but banged a few pots around. Alice tried again.

"Thank you for my new clothes and for letting me go to school, mother. I will make you proud. I am good at learning."

Eliza didn't even glance at her but she put a slightly bigger plate of food in front of Alice.

"You'll see the schoolhouse, it's straight down that road. Go on now and don't dally home. You got chores that need doing."

Alice strolled away from the house but once she thought she was out of view, she ran. She would see other children and make friends. It took a while to reach the town but thankfully the schoolhouse was on this side.

She didn't see any children. Was she late? Heart hammering against her chest, she walked up the steps and knocked. A child answered it with a smile which disappeared as a voice boomed out.

"Who is it, Peter? Don't stand there, come in. You're letting all the heat out."

"It's a girl, Mr. Bell, never seen her before."

ORPHAN TRAIN STRIKE

"Come inside and shut that door."

Alice stepped into the room as the children all turned to face her. Some smiled, others remained stoney faced but two girls laughed. "Look at what she's wearing. It looks like an old sack from father's shop."

Alice colored, waiting for the teacher to tell the girl to stop but he didn't speak. Her blonde haired, blue-eyed tormentor wore the most beautiful dress Alice had ever seen. A shade of blue the color of the sea in the books Miss Baker had shared with her. Alice crossed her hands in front of her, as if to hide the dress. The girl's smirk grew bigger. Alice couldn't bear the look of disdain in her face.

She switched her gaze to the teacher, a tall thin man with a receding hairline and the biggest whiskers she had ever seen. He looked like old pictures of Abraham Lincoln. She jumped at his squeaky high-pitched voice.

"And what time do you call this? School started thirty minutes ago."

"Sorry Sir, I didn't know. I'm new to town." Alice could feel everyone staring at her but she stared at a point above the man's head. She didn't like the look in his eyes either.

"You're the orphan girl aren't you?"

window. Matron had given Dawn permission to go see it and allowed her to take one girl. Alice had been so excited. She licked her lips at the memories of the roasted chestnuts she'd eaten. Dawn said the seller gave them to her, but Alice wasn't sure that was true. Dawn had been very good at getting things from strangers, especially men.

She wondered what Dawn was doing now. She hoped she was happy. What would Dawn do if she lived in this house? How she wished someone was here with her, even Issy would be welcome. Why couldn't she have been part of a big family with brothers and sisters?

CHAPTER 10

As the weeks flew past, Maria found it got harder to go to work each morning. She wanted to stay snuggled up in bed with her sisters keeping her warm.

Flurries of snow made people crankier despite it getting closer to Christmas. They had to break the ice on the water in the morning to wash their faces. When Mama heard Rosa complain it was too cold, she called.

"It's good for your skin, tighten it up."

Rosa mimicked their mother the whole way to work making Maria laugh. Working at the factory was hard but at least she had Rosa looking out for her. She also got to see a different part of town.

Sometimes they walked down Fifth Avenue just to see how the rich people behaved.

"Look at that window, Rosa. That hat would look lovely on Mama. Imagine her wearing that to mass."

"It's red. Mama only wears black to church."

That was true but Maria didn't stop dreaming of gifts to brighten her parents' Christmas. She loved looking at the different stores and stalls. Despite the cold, the stall holders decorated their small stalls hoping to attract the Christmas trade.

It was fun to have a couple of coins to treat her family. She gave all her wages to mama but papa had insisted she keep a few cents for herself.

"Mama, the girls work hard. They must enjoy a little from their wages. Don't you think?" Papa winked at Maria as he spoke but didn't let his wife see him.

Maria wasn't sure mama agreed but mama never said no to Papa.

"Maria, buy something to keep your hair tidy. It looks like a bird's nest." Despite her words, mama's voice was warm so Maria knew her mother was protesting for the sake of it. She couldn't let her children see any weakness.

"Yes, mama." She leaned over to kiss her

father's cheek. "Thank you, Papa." She choked out the thanks as she noticed he winced in pain. She hadn't meant to hurt him.

"Maria, my pet you didn't hurt me. It's the cold. I feel it in my bones. I prayed for a little sunshine."

Maria couldn't answer. Dear Papa, he didn't deserve to be in pain all the time. Their apartment felt too small, and she struggled to breathe or at least that's what it felt like.

"Mama, can I take Louisa and Sophia out to see the store windows? They dress them up for Christmas."

"I don't know, they should do their homework."

Papa intervened again to save them. "Mama, let the girls go. Maria will take care of them. They are good children. Go on now."

Louisa threw herself at Mama giving her a hug. "Please Mama, my homework is all done. At school the teacher told us about Macy's. Some others have seen it already. Please, mama."

"Go on with you. But mind you listen to Maria. Be home before it's dark."

"Yes, Mama."

Maria didn't wait for her mother to change her mind. She rushed the girls out the door. At the last minute Rosa joined them and for once Maria didn't mind. She was getting on well with her sister, working together brought them closer.

They brought home a small tree. Despite Mama's protests the apartment was too small, she helped them to decorate the tree. The younger girls made paper decorations while Rosa baked gingerbread cookies, letting her sisters roll out the dough. The scent of sugar cooking, ginger and the pines from the tree filled the small space.

"Louisa put some of those cookies on the tree before your sisters eat them all."

"Yes, Mama but Papa likes them too."

Mama pretended to scold Papa for taking another cookie but the girls saw she was joking. Papa broke the stolen cookie in half and gave it to his wife. "Here, share mine."

"You are too generous," Mama replied.

"Now you can get fat too."

The girls giggled as Mama playfully hit Papa over the head with a towel.

CHAPTER 11

Christmas was Alice's favorite time of the year and she couldn't help but get excited.

"Mother will we have a Christmas tree?"

"Alice, what type of family do you think we are?"

"I never seen one, not up close I mean. We used to see them through the windows of some houses in New York."

"Mr. Ackerman always picks the nicest tree. Cuts it down and brings it home himself."

"Can I help you get it ready?"

"We'll see how you behave, Alice. You tore a hole in your new dress yesterday."

* * *

She drove Eliza mad asking when he would be home with the tree but she couldn't help it. Her excitement bubbled over. She spotted him outside and ran down the stairs to open the door to let him in.

"Doesn't it smell lovely?" Alice said, forgetting the rule about adults speaking first. He turned on her with fury.

"Get out of my sight. Get to bed, there's no supper for you tonight."

Alice ran, not bothering to explain. He'd spanked her the last time she'd answered back as he called it.

She lay in bed shivering with cold, terrified he would change his mind and come up to spank her, but he didn't. She fell asleep cold and hungry but thankful she could still sit down. She had to try harder not to upset them.

The next morning, she was up and dressed before her mother called her. She saw him go out in the wagon and only then did she make her way downstairs. They would decorate the tree today. It was Christmas Eve.

"There you are. Get your coat on and collect some wood for the fire. Ned forgot to fill up the buckets and I am too busy."

Disappointed but too scared to argue, Alice grabbed her coat and gloves and headed outside. Collecting wood for the fire took ages as the bucket was too big and heavy for her to carry so she had to bring in the wood piece by piece.

By the time she finished, the decorations were up.

Alice looked in wonder at the Christmas tree taking pride of place in the Ackerman's. She'd never seen one up close before and reached out her hand to touch it only for Eliza to slap it away.

"Don't touch girl, it's taken me all day to get it looking this good."

"You did a wonderful job, Eliza. It will be the envy of all your friends. Those cookies look good enough to eat." Ned Ackerman took one of the sugar-coated gingerbread ornaments from the nearest branch. Breaking it in two he held out half to Alice.

She took a step forward, the scent of ginger and cinnamon assailing her nostrils making her mouth water. Just as she reached out to take the offering, he shoved it into his mouth. "You heard your mother, no touching."

Alice let her hand fall to her side. It was pointless to argue. He wouldn't listen. She glanced at the presents wrapped under the tree. Was one of them for her?

"Off to bed with you now. Church is at ten tomorrow morning and I won't be late."

"Am I coming to Church with you?" Alice whispered, her attention on her feet. Eliza didn't like her to look at her face.

"No, Alice, Wolf will keep you company."

Hearing his name, the large half wolf, half dog snarled at them, baring his teeth. Alice tried to contain her shivering. If the Ackerman's knew just how terrified she was of the newest addition to the family, they would take delight in torturing her.

"Go to bed, Alice."

"Yes Mother, goodnight."

Alice left the room, taking her time on the stairs where the light shone. Her room would be cold and dark. She didn't dare complain or ask for another blanket. She'd made that mistake one time too many. After saying her prayers and washing her face, she undressed and got into bed. Curling up in a ball, she pushed her face into her pillow and only then did the tears fall. Closing her eyes, she could see blurry images of a man and a woman, she liked to think they were her parents smiling.

CHAPTER 12

NEW YORK, CHRISTMAS EVE 1906

"Time's up." Reinhardt glanced at his watch. "The boss let you go home early for Christmas. Go on, out. I have a drink waiting for me across the road."

Maria didn't need Reinhardt to tell them twice. She jumped out of her chair ready to go. She wished Mrs. Stein a happy Christmas but as soon as the words were out of her mouth, she apologized.

"Don't apologize young Maria. I may not celebrate Christmas like your family, but I like the tradition. Just don't tell my Rabbi." Mrs. Stein smiled, her eyes dancing. She handed Maria a small gift, wrapped in brown paper.

Maria flushed. "What is this?"

"It is something small. I think you will like it. A

reminder of home to make you smile." Mrs. Stein smiled. "Yes?"

Maria opened the package to reveal a small but perfectly formed lemon. She brushed the tears from her eyes before giving Mrs. Stein a hug.

"Papa will love this. Thank you. I'm sorry, I didn't think."

"Maria don't worry. Your smile is all I need. Now go, your sister is waiting."

Mrs. Stein turned away leaving Maria to stare at the lemon.

"A lemon? Where did you get that?" Rosa asked as she came over to scold her for dawdling.

"Mrs. Stein gave it to me. Wasn't she kind?"

"Kind? What did she want?"

Maria glanced toward Mrs. Stein but thankfully she was close to the exit and so couldn't hear Rosa.

"Rosa Mezza, what do you have against Mrs. Stein?"

"She's a Jew." Rosa picked up Maria's bag. "Are you ready to go?"

Tempted to go home, Maria wavered. They had plans to go to the market to get Papa tobacco and some candies for the girls.

"Hurry, Maria. I need to collect Paulo's present." Rosa picked up the lemon. "I guess it was kind of her to bring you a gift. It makes me think of home and grandmother."

Stunned to see a tear glistening on Rosa's eyelash, Maria forgot her rage.

"We should buy some writing paper and write to grandmother."

"Good idea, she must be lonely, I miss her."

They walked out of the building arm in arm, both shivering as the cold air hit them on exiting. Maria huddled closer to Rosa for warmth. "Will you help me finish Mama's scarf? She might wear it to Midnight mass."

Rosa put her arm through Maria's. "What are sisters for?"

The two of them had good fun and treated themselves to a hot drink from one of the decorated stalls before they got home. Mama was cooking many things and shouting in Italian, so they escaped to the room they shared with their younger siblings.

"Mama always gets over excited and cooks enough to feed the universe." Rosa commented as she put the packages on the bed.

"You know the heat gets to her plus she likes to cook a little extra to give to the poorer families. It makes her happy."

Rosa frowned.

"What's wrong with you?" Maria asked.

"Nothing."

"Rosa, tell me now or I will tell Mama you bought Paulo gloves. She will make you take them back."

"You wouldn't."

Maria wouldn't but she wanted to know what was upsetting her sister.

"I just worry about Mama and Papa. It's been so long since Papa had a real job. I know they worry about money and yet mama pretends everything is okay."

Maria had heard their mama and papa talking late at night too, but she knew her parents would turn things around. So long as the family were together, that was all that mattered.

"Don't think like that Rosa. It's Christmas tomorrow. So, what did you buy me? Your favorite working sister?"

"You're my only working sister, Grignolla!"

Maria tickled Rosa in reply to her calling her a greenhorn. Soon they were rolling around like two children not almost grown women. Louisa and Sophie joined in and soon the sound of laughter dominated the apartment. Mama shouted at them to keep the noise down, but her voice didn't sound angry.

Maria knew she was happy. Benito, her eldest brother and mama's favorite son and his pregnant wife would come tomorrow for dinner. All was well in the Mezza household.

After their return from midnight mass, Maria slept with the lemon under her pillow. She would give it to papa in the morning but for now, she wanted to savor its scent. She fell asleep dreaming of their old farm, the sun on her face, surrounded with fresh sea air.

CHAPTER 13

DEADMAN'S CREEK, CHRISTMAS MORNING, 1906

Alice jumped out of bed, hoping from one foot to the other as her toes hit the cold floor. She dressed as fast as she could and had her bed made in no time. Maybe if Eliza saw how good she was, she would let her go to Church with her new family.

The smell of bacon wafted up the stairs. A cooked breakfast! They used to have those back in the orphanage when important visitors were coming or on special occasions like Christmas. Alice ran down the stairs and into the kitchen.

"What have I told you about running? You must walk like a lady."

"Yes, Mother, Happy Christmas."

But her greeting went unanswered. Eliza

finished cooking breakfast before calling to her husband to join them. He didn't acknowledge Alice but took his seat at the head of the table. Eliza heaped the food on her husband's plate and then on her own. For a couple of horrible seconds, Alice thought Eliza would not give her anything to eat. It wouldn't be the first time, but this was Christmas Day. Her worries were unfounded as Eliza put two pieces of bacon, a fried tomato and some beans on her plate.

Ned said grace and then they began to eat.

"We will give out presents after Church, don't you agree Mother?"

Eliza nodded while Alice panicked. She didn't have any presents for these people. She hadn't been near Clayton's store. Not that it mattered as she didn't have any money. Her eyes darted from one to another until Eliza dropped her knife and fork on the table.

"What is the matter with you?" she asked Alice.

"I'm sorry but I don't have any presents for you. I...well I don't have any money to buy something."

He looked at her making her skin crawl. "I'm sure you will reconsider your selfishness while Mother and I are at church. As the Bible says, where there is a will, there is a way." He went back to chewing loudly following each mouthful with a drink of coffee.

Alice swallowed hard. What did he expect her to do?

She cleared the table and did the dishes while they went to church. She ran outside trying to find some flowers or something to give Eliza as a Christmas present, but it was pointless. Although it wasn't snowing like a New York winter, frost covered the ground. Despondent, she returned to the warmth of the kitchen. She spotted a pencil and some paper lying on the shelf. Eliza used them to make notes of things she wanted in the store.

Alice hummed as she drew her picture. She was good at drawing, well so the teachers back in New York had said. She drew a picture of a family with a mother, a father and a cat. She added herself in last.

Feeling pretty pleased with herself, she went upstairs to change into some old clothes to do her chores in the barn. She had to collect the Eggs. As Alice approached the barn, Wolf growled. Alice stood frozen to the spot.

Her heart thumped as he came toward her, his mouth open showing sharp looking teeth. Alice's eyes darted between the barn and the house. Could she run faster than the animal? He growled again.

She dropped the egg basket and ran. Wolf sprang into action and ran after her. Just as she reached the barn door, he caught her. She tumbled over her own feet at the impact, screaming waiting for his teeth to sink into her arm but he nudged her. Then he licked her. She giggled as it tickled. He licked her again and again before lying on the ground beside her. When she didn't move, he nudged her hand with his head.

"What?" she asked him, heart still hammering.

His dark eyes, almost black, looked up at her before he butted her hand once more. She held it open and he licked it and then the other. "Do you smell the bacon?"

Alice jumped up and ran back into the house. Although she knew she was alone in the house, she still glanced around. How could she give Wolf some bacon without it being noticed? Glancing around her once more, she took two of the smallest pieces of the left-over bacon, rearranging the other cut pieces to hide her theft. She ran back outside to where Wolf was waiting. He jumped up and snatched the bacon from her hand but didn't hurt her.

She patted his head. Every time she stopped, he butted against her to do it again. Giggling, she found a stick and threw it. Wolf retrieved it, dropping it at her feet. He panted as the drool dropped from his mouth until Alice threw the stick again. They played for ages and gradually Alice lost all fear of the animal.

The dog's ears perked up, and he started growling. Alice tried to throw the stick, but it only made him growl more. He ran toward the house looking behind him. When she didn't follow, he ran back and around her before heading to the house again.

"Do you want more bacon? I don't have any?" she said.

But he wasn't listening. He seemed to want her to go inside the house. Then she heard the wagon. The Ackerman's were coming back. She ran inside, up the stairs and changed into her Christmas clothes. She was back downstairs waiting in the kitchen by the time the couple came inside.

"Did you have a nice time?" she asked.

"We are at Church not a country fair." Eliza snapped back.

Alice picked up the picture and gave it to the woman. "Happy Christmas Mother."

Eliza took the picture but handed it to her husband without looking at it. He smiled causing the hair on the back of Alice's neck to rise. She did something wrong but what?

"You get permission to use the paper and pencil?" he asked, not raising his voice.

"No Father, I hoped Mother wouldn't mind. You said I should have a present for her. There were no flowers outside, and I didn't know what else to..." her excuses trailed off as he stared at her. She took a step back.

"We will discuss stealing tomorrow. It's Christmas Day and I won't ruin it for your mother."

Alice quivered. She hadn't stolen the paper. She didn't ask permission, but it was just a small piece of paper. She didn't say a word.

Eliza wouldn't let her help in the kitchen, so she sat on the porch despite the cold. Wolf growled and kept his distance. Her eyes stung with tears. Why was the dog behaving that way?

They ate dinner in silence the same as always. After, she picked up the dishes and washed them. Eliza scolded her for not doing them properly, so she started over. It took her two hours to get everything the way Eliza liked it. He was sitting by the fire in the next room reading the Bible while Eliza was knitting. She made them a cup of tea and then waited for them to tell her what to do.

She didn't like the so-called best room, but the fire made it brighter than usual. Everything was brown, the walls, the floors and even the rug in front of the fireplace. She wondered if brown was Eliza's favorite color as her dresses were always dark too.

"Would you like your present?" he asked without looking up from his reading. She looked behind her before she realized he was talking to her. Her stomach bubbled as if there were a load of little people inside jumping around. They had bought her a present for Christmas. Would it be an orange? She loved oranges and Miss Baker had always given each girl one at Christmas. Or she had last year. Alice didn't remember the Christmas before that. Miss Baker said it was because she'd been ill after bumping her head badly in an accident. Her father coughed causing Alice to look at him. He was waiting.

"Yes, please."

He stared at her over the rim of the book.

"I forgot. Please, Father."

"Mother, give her the box."

Eliza put her knitting down and gave Alice a large box covered in brown paper but with a pink bow wrapped around it. The bow was pretty. Alice's mouth grew dry as her heart raced with excitement. Would it be a doll? She loved Agatha but another doll would be good. She could have a tea party with two dolls.

"Go on, open it."

She restrained the urge to tear the paper off. Instead, she opened the bow carefully and folded the paper before she looked for permission to open the box. Real dolls came in boxes. She had seen some in the store window in town. One had curly brown hair and a beautiful dress.

Alice hadn't expected a present but now she couldn't help hoping it was.... a leather strap. She glanced at him before looking back in the package. The big box contained a leather strap. Unbelieving, she picked it up, putting it to one side and looked in the box for her present. She knew it was stupid to look but still she did. She glanced at him, tears blurring her vision.

"What do you say?" he asked.

She glanced at the strap and then back at the man who made her call him Father. Why was he being so horrible? She choked back tears, her voice shaking.

"Thank you, Father."

"Go hang it on the hook in the kitchen. That way we know where it's at when it's needed."

Alice stumbled as she tried to sit up.

"Go on, girl. Do as you are told."

She staggered to the kitchen trying to keep her hurt inside. The hook was too high for her to reach. He'd followed her. "Let me help you with that."

He lifted her up so she could reach and held her as she put the strap on the hook. Then he let her fall. She fell on the floor. He walked into the front room closing the door behind him. Alice sat on the floor in the darkness, her head on her arms, her whole-body shuddering as the tears came. She heard Wolf growl outside.

CHAPTER 14

JUNE 1909

Alice winced at the sound his boots made as they walked toward her bedroom. Almost two and a half years had passed since she had come to this house but in that time, things had got worse not better. That first Christmas had been horrible but only a taste of what was to come. She could never please the people who were now her parents.

He'd been drinking, his steps unsteady as he hit the wall a couple of times as he made his way up the stairs. She buried deeper under the scratchy blue rug covering her bed. Please God let him leave her alone. She closed her eyes, hoping he'd believe she was asleep. Maybe then he would take pity on her and leave her be. She heard his heavy breathing at the door. Despite wanting to pretend to be asleep, her eyes focused on the handle. She watched it move downward at the same time the door screeched as the rusty hinge protested.

"Girl come here. Mother has told me how badly you behaved today. I'll teach ya to show respect to your betters, you no good ungrateful wretch. Come here, I say, or you'll regret it."

She pushed under the blanket and shut her eyes. The stench of whiskey hit her nostrils. She didn't understand why he hated her so much. They'd picked her from the train. They could have chosen any of several children. She pushed herself into the mattress trying to put distance between them.

"Don't think you'll get away from me this time, girl. Get out of that bed now. You know what to do, over there by the chair."

She squinted at his hands, shivering at the sight of the strap, her first Christmas present. She darted a glance at the door, could she make a run for it? Even as the thought crossed her mind, his hairy hand grabbed her shoulder.

"You never learn do you, girl? Never showing gratitude to us, your real parents who saved you from the bad ways of your family."

He pulled her from the bed, her foot sliding

against the floor to put off the torture ahead of her. But it was useless. With one hand, he picked her up and threw her down on the chair. With the other he tore the nightgown from her back. Mother would punish her tomorrow for tearing yet another item of clothing.

Alice was responsible. It was her fault he drank and if she misbehaved, he'd beat her. Alice never knew what behavior would warrant a beating. It changed from one day to the next. She racked her brains to find a reason for this one. She'd finished her chores and watered the garden front and back. She'd even weeded the vegetable patch.

As the strap descended, she braced herself for impact. She couldn't cry. She'd learned long ago that would make things worse. She forced herself to think of New York. Some day she would return to the city of her birth and find her real father. In her fantasy, she could see a man running toward her, his face lit up with a kind smile as tears flowed down his cheeks. "Alice, my darling daughter, you are home," he would say and then he would tell her it was all a mistake. The blows continued as she tried to blot out his words, they were almost worse.

"You worthless, ungrateful wretch." And then the blackness came.

* * *

THE NEXT MORNING, she woke in a huddle on the floor. Her skin screamed with pain. She pulled herself to her feet, her teeth almost piercing her lip in a bid not to cry out. She listened to the sounds of the house. Was he still here or had he left already? It was Monday so he should be away for the next four, maybe five days. She and Eliza would be alone in the house.

On the rare occasion Eliza took her to town, the people used to comment on how Alice was as pretty as a picture and how lucky she was to have such wonderful parents. Alice wanted to protest, to show these people the bruises under her clothes. The welts on her back that never healed. But she couldn't. They wouldn't believe her. She was an orphan train child and the Ackermans, well they were real town's folk.

She pulled the cover up over her pillow making the bed as neat looking as she could. The blanket was almost threadbare, the floor still bare wood.

"Alice, get downstairs now." Alice winced as she tried to get dressed without hurting her back more. She pulled on a brown pinafore dress and put her hair up just as Eliza had shown her. Despite it being summer, Eliza insisted she wear the same brown dress she'd worn to school.

"Alice! Don't have me come up there to get you. I've got to go to town today."

Alice hurried to wash her face and with a glance in the mirror she walked downstairs trying to hold her back straight.

"There you are. Come here and let me fix your hair."

She stayed silent as Eliza fixed her hair, dragging the brush painfully through the long blonde tresses.

"Pity you are so ugly. If only God had graced, you with a pleasant face and disposition. I guess he decided you had to pay for your parents' sins."

"Yes, Mother." Alice responded automatically. She agreed with everything Eliza said, knowing if she didn't, she would get a pinch or worse.

"I don't know what time I will be home but it will be late. I've left you a cold supper."

Alice stilled her face not wanting her mother to guess how excited she was to have a day to herself.

"Make sure you do your chores."

"Yes, Mother, have a nice day."

"I'm helping dear Mrs. Clayton birth her baby not having fun. The Bible says help thy neighbor."

What about loving the children but Alice wasn't about to ask? She waited until Eliza had walked down to the main road before she whooped for joy. She had the whole day to herself. She'd go swimming in the creek. Wolf would enjoy that.

Her chores done in record time, Alice released Wolf.

"Come on boy, we're going swimming."

Wolf barked and ran around. Giggling Alice raced to the creek. She'd found a sunny spot with a nice rock to sunbathe on. The water was perfect for cooling off when the sun got too hot. She didn't swim as she didn't know how but she walked out to chest level. Wolf swam around her.

Wolf barked.

"What is it?" she glanced around but couldn't see anything. Wolf barked again and then someone whistled.

Chills went down her spine. Had he come home early?

It was worse.

"Hey, it's Alice, that stuck up girl from class. You know the one who never talks to us."

Alice had nearly drowned trying to hide under the water. She didn't want anyone to see her, least of all the newest boys in school. Twins they were and they teased everyone.

"Watch out, Alice. There's a croc in the water."

Alice didn't hesitate but tore out of the water like her hair was on fire. Only then did she realize they had caught her with another one of their jokes.

Water dripped off her as she protested, "That was cruel."

Wolf sniffed and barked at the boys but when they threw him a stick, he retrieved it. Some friend he was.

"Alice, you got to be stupid if you think there are crocodiles in that water, it ain't warm enough."

She didn't know which boy had spoken to her given they were identical.

"You're just mean."

Without thinking, she turned her back on them. Silence.

"Alice, what's on your back?"

Alice cringed. Her shirt had come loose, and they'd seen her skin.

"None of your business. Go away."

One of them, Jack she later found out, came closer. "Alice, we're sorry. We shouldn't have done that. But nobody should hit a girl. Who did that to you?"

She moved back from him, holding her dry clothes up in front of her as some barrier.

"Nobody," Alice's heart hammered. She'd be in all kinds of trouble if the Ackerman's found out anyone had seen her wounds. "Please, just go."

"Nope." The boy sat down and his brother followed his example.

Alice glanced around her. Trapped between the boys and the water behind her, she begged them to leave her be.

"Come on Alice, you'll get cold. Tell us what happened. We'll help ya won't we, Jack?"

Anger filled Jack's face. She stared at him and he back at her. She looked to Jacob. "I'll get in trouble."

"Ned Ackerman did it."

Alice and Jacob looked at Jack. He stood up. "Jacob come on, walk ahead until Alice gets dressed and then we will walk her home."

Alice didn't confirm or deny his comment but got dressed and followed them. They didn't make any further comment about the scars on her back but walked her to the edge of the homestead.

"Can you get out again tomorrow, Alice? Me and Jack, we're going fishing. You can come too if you like?"

ORPHAN TRAIN STRIKE

Alice nodded. "I might get away."

"We'll be up along there, see where our poles are?" Jacob pointed to a place further up the creek. "You come when you're ready."

Alice couldn't believe it. She had friends. Well one, Jacob. The other boy looked too angry to be anyone's friend.

Wolf, forgiven for playing with the boys, ran around her feet, tripping her up and playing. When she got home, the house was empty. Something she welcomed. She ate her meal, tidied up and headed to her bedroom. She wanted to re-live the day over again.

The next morning Eliza had still not returned. Alice did her chores and then waited. Could she risk going fishing but what if Mother came home?

She'd dressed up in her oldest clothes when the front door banged. Shaking she opened her bedroom door to hear Eliza calling for her.

"I'm here, Mother."

"Good grief, what are you dressed like that for?"

Alice looked at her clothes. "I thought I might try to find some berries for a pie. I knew you would be hungry and might like some."

Eliza's eyes widened with distrust but Alice held her gaze. Eliza sighed.

"I am tried. It would be nice to have the house to myself without you making noise. Go on then but don't wander too far."

"Thank you, Mother."

Alice ran, not giving Eliza a chance to change her mind.

She didn't take Wolf with her as she knew Eliza would be suspicious. As soon as she was out of sight of the house, she ran to the spot where the boys were fishing.

"Hi ya Alice. Jack just caught supper. Look at this."

"Can you show me how to do that?"

"It's all about the worms." Jack, patiently showed her all his tricks.

Alice sat for ages with the rod in the water but nothing happened.

"They don't like me."

"Don't be silly, they don't know ya. You're shaking the stick so much they think there's a hurricane coming. You got to have patience." Jacob said before standing up. "I'm starving."

Jacob handed Alice some bread with cheese and ham inside. "Mam gave us this for you."

"She did?"

"But if you ain't hungry, I'll eat it. I'm always starving."

Alice held the sandwich tight. She was hungry. She bit into it savoring each bite.

"Jeez do girls always take so long to eat?" Jacob grumbled. "Want a drink?"

Alice nodded.

Jacob pulled a container from the water. "Keeps it cool, see?"

Alice took a gulp of cold milk. This was easily the best day of her life.

"You got to taste Ma's apple pie. She makes the best. Does your ma make you pie?"

"Sometimes." She took the piece of pie he offered and grinned.

From that day, their relationship had changed. She later found out, they'd told their Pa about the marks on her back, but he hadn't believed them, and they got a leathering for telling lies about their elders. But their ma believed them. At least they thought she did as she always included something for Alice in the twin's lunch pails. She said nothing to Alice or to the Ackermans. Alice would have known if she had as she knew her miserable life would have only gotten worse.

CHAPTER 15

AUGUST 1909, FAIRFIELDS HOSPITAL, NEW YORK

Maria Mezza shifted in the chair trying to get comfortable. She was too hot. Everywhere was stifling. She'd sent mama home, to Rosa who was minding their little sisters. Once Rosa got Mama to eat, her sister would come back to the hospital to relieve Maria. Doctor Green was kind, he said they could have someone with papa all the time now.

Maria knew that meant the doctor thought Papa was dying. Otherwise they would have to keep the same visiting hours as the other patients. She'd heard the nurses sending people home despite the people begging to stay with a family member. A sole tear slipped down her cheek. Papa didn't deserve to be lying here on a hospital bed in New

York. He should be back in Sicily, where he'd been happy.

"Are you okay? Would you like a drink?"

The nurse's gentle inquiry made Maria jump, causing the nurse to apologize.

"I'm sorry I didn't mean to startle you. But you just looked so sad and alone, I thought you might like some company."

As she spoke the girl checked Papa, taking his pulse and listening to his breathing.

"He is doing better isn't he?"

Surprised Maria inched forward. "Do you really think so? I thought Dr. Green said he was dying?"

"No, he is definitely improving. Dr. Green explained he got over the crisis at the night before last. He thinks your father will survive this bout, Miss Mezza."

"My name is Maria." Maria held out her hand. "Thank you, nurse."

"Frieda, I'm not a nurse but a trainee doctor. I'm studying and Dr. Green allows me to help him look after his patients. I can't do much more than the nurses do to be fair but at least it gets me away from the books. He's a wonderful doctor. Your father is in good hands."

Maria could barely follow what Frieda was

saying as the woman spoke fast. But it wasn't just the fact she spoke English with a trace of an accent but what she was saying. A woman doctor.

"Are you feeling all right, you are pale." Frieda asked.

"Are you really going to be a doctor? I never heard of lady doctors before."

"Yes, I really am. There aren't many but there have been a few including some rather famous ones."

"How did you become a doctor if you don't mind me asking?"

"Why don't I get us both a hot drink and come back and tell you?"

"Please." Maria didn't want to sound desperate even though she was. If you could become a woman doctor in America, she could do something. She would not work in a factory for the rest of her life and end up like Mrs. Stein. Poor woman, she'd lost her job and her home. Maria remembered her kindness and the lemon she'd given her for Papa. If only she had some lemons now, she could make Papa a drink from them. It reminded him of grandma. She blinked a few times. Now was not the time to think about grandma. This time last year she'd been alive.

"There you are. Be careful, it's hot. Not the best coffee but it will warm you up. Has he woken yet?"

Maria shook her head, suddenly shy. She couldn't believe she had asked such an intimate question.

"What do you work at Maria?"

"I'm a machinist. I make shirtwaists much like the one you're wearing." Maria's English faltered because of nerves.

Frieda fingered the material of her blouse. "My friends made this one for me. I'm lucky. Lily, that's the lady who owns the house where I live, has some seamstresses working for her. They make all my clothes. I'm not good at sewing. Apart from stitching people up."

Smiling at the joke, Maria warmed to the kind woman even more. She didn't think there was much in age difference between them although Frieda was older.

"So, you asked how I ended up studying to be a doctor. Are you interested in medicine?"

"No, can't bear the sight of blood. I just wondered. You know you hear everything is possible in America but when you come here you find out…"

"You realize the streets aren't gold and you

might end up working harder and being worse off than you were at home?"

Maria grinned as Frieda put Maria's exact thoughts into words. "You've heard it before?"

"I've lived it. My family came here from Germany. Papa thought we would have a better life. And I do."

Maria heard Frieda's voice break, saw a flash of pain in her expression. She put her hand out wanting to offer comfort but let it fall again as Frieda continued talking.

"There are opportunities but it helps to have good people looking out for you."

"Your papa must be a modern man to allow his daughter to be a doctor." Maria regretted her words as soon as they spilled out of her mouth. Really, she should learn to stay silent. "I'm sorry. That was rude of me."

"My father believed girls should stay at home, grow up to become wives and mothers. I think he would be rather shocked to see me here. Like this."

Frieda had changed her father's mind. Maybe she could give Maria some tips on dealing with Papa. She wanted to ask but didn't want to interrupt her new friend.

"A few years ago, my father and brother died.

You may not have heard about it, but a boat sank on the River. We were on it. I survived." Frieda spoke so softly, Maria could barely hear the words, but she heard the pain. She reached out her hand and squeezed Frieda's. "I'm sorry. I didn't mean to remind you of your pain. I can't imagine losing a sibling, can't bear to think about losing Papa."

"It's been five years now, this past June. I can't believe it's been that long, some days it seems like yesterday."

A young man in a nice suit interrupted them. Maria had seen him earlier, the nurse had called him doctor.

"Freida, there you are. Can you help...oh I apologize I didn't mean to interrupt?"

Maria watched with interest how Frieda face flushed as the young doctor spoke. She wondered if she was in trouble.

"Sorry Doctor it was me. Frieda gave me some good news and kept me company. If she is in trouble, it's my fault."

The doctor laughed. "Frieda's not in any trouble. Dad was looking for her as she has the steadiest hand for dealing with young children. Frieda, do you mind?"

"Not at all." Frieda replied, glancing at the

young man before turning her attention back to Maria. " Maria, get some rest. Your father will be much better in the morning."

Maria didn't have time to say thanks as Frieda moved so fast. She caught the young doctor staring after her.

"Sorry Miss, I wouldn't have interrupted only dad has some fixed ideas."

"We were just talking about fathers. Frieda was just telling me about her family."

The young doctor looked in the direction Frieda had taken but the woman had disappeared.

"Poor thing, I thought she looked a little upset. It was a bad business and preventable too. That boat shouldn't have been out on the water. If it wasn't for Frieda and her brother, more would have died. They were heroes, both of them. Sorry I didn't introduce myself. Doctor to be, Patrick Green."

"Green? Your father is looking after Papa?"

"Yes, that would be him. How is your father doing?"

"Better after seeing your father. I thought, we all thought he was…"

"Dying! They had my coffin all measured up, young man."

"Papa! Don't say things like that." Maria

couldn't scold him for long. She gave him a kiss and held onto his hand. "You scared us. Mama was here all night. I came straight from work and sent her home."

"You are a good girl Maria." Papa looked at the young man. "Your father is a wonderful doctor, you should be very proud."

Patrick examined her father as he chatted.

"I am, he is fantastic. But it wasn't just him. Frieda, the lady your daughter met is an asset to the hospital, she nursed you through the worst of the crisis."

"Yes, a fine nurse." Papa nodded although Maria knew he hadn't a clue who Patrick was talking about.

"Papa, not a nurse but a doctor. She's studying to become a doctor. In America, anything is possible. You told us that, Papa."

Papa didn't respond but Maria knew he'd heard her from his expression. He looked thoughtful. "Her father, he allowed this?" Papa directed his question to Patrick.

"He didn't have a say. He died over five years ago in the General Slocum disaster." Patrick told them how Frieda and her family and neighbors had gone to the picnic and the events of the day. "I have a little sister called Elsa thanks to Frieda's brother. He saved her at the cost of his own life."

"She is a good woman, this Frieda." Papa stumbled over the German name. "I would like to thank her for looking after me so well."

"Dad, I mean Doctor Green called for her to assist him with a young child. She's remarkable with the younger patients too. They trust her straight away."

Maria hid a smile. His interest in Frieda wasn't purely professional. She wondered if they each had admitted how they felt. It was so romantic.

"Maria, go home now and tell your mama to rest. I will see you tomorrow after Mass."

Her papa couldn't be that ill, he hadn't lost track of the days. Still she would prefer to be with him than listening to Father Anthonio.

"But Papa,"

"Maria Josephina Mezza, do as you are told."

With a look at Patrick, Maria agreed. "Yes, Papa." She kissed his cheek and left but with a lighter step than she had arrived. When Papa used her full name, you knew his temper was up and that took energy. Energy he didn't have a few nights ago.

As she walked home, she thought of Frieda. She

was an incredible woman, not only because she was studying to be a doctor but she seemed to be doing it as an orphan. She would like to get to know Frieda better. And find out more about her and Patrick. Giggling she told herself off for being too romantic. Mama said it came from reading the American books her teacher had given her. Papa just smiled and said all Sicilians were romantics at heart and kissed Mama to stop her disagreeing.

CHAPTER 16

*A*lice saw the Denton twins waiting for her on the road. Jacob greeted her, arm outstretched. She could tell the difference between them now. Jack had a large mole just above his right ear.

"Here Alice, Ma said to give you this. She made it yesterday, but it's still nice."

Ma Denton was a kind, hardworking woman who smiled all the time despite being married to a man who everyone knew drank too much and was always getting into one scrape after another. The twins had several siblings all older than them. They were the surprise babies, born when their ma was about to become a grandma.

"Thanks Jacob." Alice put the whole slice of pie

into her mouth, in case someone would take it from her. "Tell your ma, that was even better than last time."

They had a real ma who smiled all the time. She was ever so kind and always made a point of greeting Alice by name if they met in town.

"Alice, one of these days you will learn not to eat it all at once."

Alice said nothing, she was too busy licking the crumbs from her hands and around her mouth. Blueberry pie was her favorite.

"The new teacher is a woman. Pa said she had no business teaching; she should be at home with her own children, but Ma told him to shut his mouth. She said Miss Lawlor would be an …," Jacob stopped for a second looking to Jack.

"Asset." Jack in contrast to Jacob didn't speak a lot. He corrected his twin when asked but otherwise seemed content to stay silent. He was happiest with his nose in a book whereas Jacob wouldn't read unless it was homework.

"Yeah that's the word, an asset. Pa didn't agree, but he didn't say nothing. He knows when Ma gets her gander up, he needs to stay silent." Jacob smiled. "Ma says Miss Lawlor is young too. Not an old bug…Ow what did you do that for?" Jacob rubbed his arm where Jack had hit him.

"Watch your mouth. You don't swear, not in front of a lady." Jack didn't look at his brother but kept his eyes straight on the road.

"I didn't swear and anyway it's only Alice. She ain't a lady are ye?" Jacob looked at Alice, a doubtful expression in his eyes. She shrugged her shoulders. She guessed not. She didn't want Jacob to treat her differently but to be her friend.

"Course she is. She's a girl and that makes her a lady."

Alice stared at Jack. It was the most she had heard him say in a long time. He went a little red, refused to look at her and stayed silent until they reached the school. Who would they find inside?

CHAPTER 17

Alice stared at the new teacher dressed in a snow-white shirtwaist with a dark blue skirt. Her hair was pulled up off her face, but already auburn tendrils had escaped and were hanging down over her freckled face. Her green eyes danced in her face as her smile lit up the room.

"Morning class, my name is April Lawlor. I would like to get to know all of you so please stand up, one at a time, tell me your name and the most important thing about you. Why don't you start?" The teacher asked Marybeth, the youngest in the class. The young girl looked around her, turned bright red and murmured.

"My name is Marybeth, I am stupid." She sat down quickly, looking at her shoes.

A frown replaced the smile on Miss Lawlor's face. Alice's stomach turned over. Was she going to shout or worse, hit Marybeth? It wasn't the young girl's fault she was slow at reading. She said the letters danced when she tried to follow the lines.

"Marybeth, it is lovely to meet you, but I never want to hear you call yourself a horrible name again. There is no such thing as a stupid child. Now would you like to start again?"

Marybeth looked around her, tears slipping down her cheeks. Alice stood up. "Please Miss Lawlor, don't be angry. Mr. Bell used to call Marybeth stupid all the time. It's not her fault. She tries hard."

"Thank you…" Miss Lawlor stared at her. Alice wasn't sure what to say until Jacob nudged her.

"You didn't tell her your name."

Alice's cheeks grew so hot, you could have fried an egg on them. "Sorry Miss, I'm Alice."

"Nice to meet you Alice. I'm not cross with you or Marybeth but I won't hear anyone call a child stupid. Marybeth, why don't you tell me something else about you?"

"I love stories." Marybeth smiled, her dimples showing. "And cookies."

Miss Lawlor's face light up. "I love cookies and stories too, they are best when they happen together."

Marybeth rubbed her stomach. "Yes, Ma'am."

Each child introduced themselves.

"My name is Alice." Alice sat down again.

"Nice to meet you again Alice but you forgot something."

Alice stood up, her stomach twisting. What could she say?

"She's an orphan train kid, nobody special." Emma Clayton shouted. Alice slid back into her seat, trying not to show anyone how hurt she was.

"Alice, please stand up and face the class."

Reluctantly Alice turned to face her classmates, forcing her feet into the floor to stop her legs from shaking. She stared at a point on the opposite wall and waited for the disparaging remarks.

"This young lady, Alice, has already shown me she has courage and a kind heart. I too traveled the Orphan Train, obviously a long time ago."

Alice turned in wonder to look at her new teacher. She could see the kindness and understanding in her eyes. At that moment she swore she would do everything in her power to make Miss Lawlor proud of her.

"Please sit, Alice." Miss Lawlor waited for her to take her seat before she frowned at the girls who had been so hurtful.

"I never want to witness unkindness like that again. Everybody deserves respect no matter what their background, or what their parents do. Do I make myself clear?"

"Yes, Miss Lawlor."

The morning flew by as Miss Lawlor checked each student's progress. She changed their seating arrangements putting students with different abilities sitting beside one another.

"We all have strengths and weaknesses. I want those who are good at English to help those who have difficulty. Those who are good at math will assist those who find it bothersome. By helping your classmates, you will reinforce your own learning, so everyone wins."

The children agreed to her proposal and soon the lunchtime bell chimed. The children flowed out of the schoolroom into the yard.

"Alice, could you stay behind please?"

"Yes, Miss Lawlor." Alice stared at her friends

as they walked out the door, chatting amongst themselves. Jack waited until everyone had left and stood at the door as if worried to leave her alone.

"Jack isn't it?" Miss Lawlor asked.

Jack nodded slowly but didn't take his eyes off Alice.

"Go on now please Jack. Alice will be fine."

Jack left albeit reluctantly. Miss Lawlor closed the door behind him and then took a seat beside Alice who took a deep breath inhaling the scent of her teacher's perfume. It smelled like Lavender with a touch of something else. She looked at her hair never having seen that color red before. She didn't realize she was staring until Miss Lawlor coughed. Alice colored.

"Where is your lunch?" Miss Lawlor asked.

Alice said nothing. She didn't want to admit she never brought lunch to school.

"I will speak to your parents. Lunch is very important to feed your mind."

Horrified, Alice quickly interrupted. "Please don't. I forgot it." She couldn't look Miss Lawlor in the face as she lied but focused on a point above her shoulder. The teacher remained silent for a few seconds, her eyes fixed on Alice's face. Alice played with her hands trying to quell the nausea in her stomach. If Miss Lawlor complained to the Ackermans, they might stop her going to school, and she loved learning.

"Alice, I will tolerate a lot of things from my students but not lies. Did you forget your lunch pail or is this a regular occurrence?"

Alice couldn't stop shaking. If she said it was, would Miss Lawlor speak to the Ackermans? If she did, Alice knew Eliza and him would blame her. She would get another whipping.

But if she lied, Miss Lawlor wouldn't like it and might get angry.

"Alice, it's a simple question. Please answer." Miss Lawlor didn't sound angry, but something told Alice she wouldn't give up until she got an answer.

"I didn't forget." Alice stared at her feet.

Miss Lawlor put her hand across the back of the seats, inadvertently touching Alice's raw shoulder. Alice jumped.

"I am so clumsy forgive me Alice. I didn't mean to hurt you."

"It's okay Miss Lawlor. Can I go outside now?" Alice was desperate to leave. She didn't want to answer any more questions.

Miss Lawlor shook her head. She stood up, walked to her desk and brought back her basket.

Alice's mouth watered at the delicious smell wafting from the small bundle, Miss Lawlor was now unwrapping.

"Alice, why don't you take half my lunch?"

Alice swallowed quickly. Although tempted to take the food, she couldn't. Miss Lawlor didn't look like she ate a lot. Maybe she was hungry too.

"I couldn't do that Miss Lawlor."

"Yes, you can, you would do me a favor. The town didn't like me living alone and insisted I take my meal with Mrs. Kavanagh. She believes I need fattening up. I would rather not end up resembling a stuffed turkey. Ian would get a fright when he arrives."

Alice's hand hovered over the offering.

"Ian miss?"

"My husband to be. He's in the army. Now let's see what Mrs. Kavanagh packed for me, shall we?"

Alice's mouth watered as Miss Lawlor put the slice of meat pie on the white handkerchief. She produced a red apple from the basket. Taking a knife, she split both the apple and pie between the two of them. They ate in silence. Perhaps Miss Lawlor sensed Alice didn't want to talk about her home life. Miss Lawlor spoke. "I hope we can become friends, Alice. Maybe one day you will trust me enough to tell me about your home. But run along now and play with your friends. Playtime is as important as lessons."

Alice stared at the teacher. Miss Lawlor was an angel sent to save her. She just knew it.

CHAPTER 18

The next morning the children rushed back to the schoolhouse to check if Miss Lawlor was still their teacher. To their joy, she was.

"Morning children. I've been thinking. This room could do with a paint couldn't it? I thought we could paint the walls white, so it makes it feel bigger. What do you think?"

Jacob spoke first. "Miss Lawlor, I don't think the Church group will like it. They will say it's too expensive."

"I can buy the paint, but I will need some helpers to paint with me. Who wants to help?"

Alice wanted to volunteer but the Ackermans wouldn't let her into town on the weekend.

"When you want it done, Miss Lawlor? My Pa gives me chores on a Saturday and Sunday is Church."

"That's very true, Marybeth. We could paint it during school. Painting walls isn't just about decorating. We get to practice our math and our geometry and maybe have fun too."

The children stared at her in unison before Jacob spoke up again. "How does throwing paint on a wall teach you about math and what was the other thing you said?"

"Geometry, which is part of math. We need to work out how much paint we need to cover the walls. We know how much the store will charge for a tin of whitewash so we will have to figure how much money it will cost to do the whole room. Now who wants to help me?"

"Me, me." Virtually everyone in the class volunteered. Alice hung back hoping Miss Lawlor wouldn't notice.

"What about you Alice? Do you like to paint?"

"I don't know, Miss Lawlor. Mother likes me to keep clean."

"Everyone will be clean. We will wear aprons and scarves over our hair. Don't worry, Alice. I will make sure I have the approval of each child's parents." Miss Lawlor clapped her hands. "Now let's get seated. I built up the fire so hopefully it will be warmer in here than yesterday. I can't abide being cold. My adoptive momma used to say I must have lived somewhere real warm when I was little. I hate being cold."

"I do too Miss Lawlor." Marybeth shivered making everyone laugh.

Miss Lawlor stood back to let everyone walk inside. As Alice passed, she said. "I will call to see your folks Alice. Don't look so worried. Everything will work out, just fine."

Alice didn't argue. Maybe, Miss Lawlor could help her.

But the visit didn't help at all, it made things worse. But for the fact Eliza had to send her to school to stop the neighbors talking, they would have confined Alice to the house. He beat her until she passed out and Eliza refused to feed her anything for the whole weekend.

On Monday, Miss Lawlor kept her inside at lunchtime.

"I made things worse didn't I, Alice? I can tell by your face. My poor girl, I'm so sorry."

Alice couldn't bear the tears in Miss Lawlor's eyes.

"No Miss Lawlor don't be sad. You care about me. Just like Miss Baker did. That makes me happy. Just please don't leave. Don't leave me here alone."

Miss Lawlor wrapped her arms around Alice and despite it hurting her wounds, Alice hugged her right back.

"I won't give up helping you Alice, I promise."

Alice stiffened.

"Don't worry Alice I will never speak to the Ackermans again. But they won't stop me."

Relieved the teacher would not try talking to her parents, Alice could breathe easy again. She ate her lunch slowly savoring every mouthful.

After lunch, Miss Lawlor gave the class a writing task while she got on with some paperwork. Alice glanced up, Miss Lawlor looked troubled as she stared into space. Then she caught Alice looking, gave her a brief smile before she put her head down and wrote. Alice couldn't help but wonder if it was something to do with her.

CHAPTER 19

CARMEL'S MISSION, NEW YORK,
SEPTEMBER 1909

*K*athleen Green walked into Lily's office removing her gloves.

"Morning Lily." Kathleen peered at Lily. "Have you been crying? You're very pale. I think you should be at home Lily."

"I'm glad you are here. We got a rather strange letter today. It's addressed to Bridget but that's all I can make out. I left my glasses at home." Lily rolled her eyes. She hated wearing them but she couldn't see without them. Vanity was not her most endearing quality.

Kathleen took the envelope and read it aloud. "Miss Lawlor, she's a teacher now but she was an orphan who traveled on the train with Bridget. Imagine her contacting us all these years later."

"What does she want?" Lily asked, wringing her hands.

"Dear Miss Bridget,

I can't remember your surname. I was a young girl on the orphan train. You said to write to you if I ever needed your help.

I was lucky. I found a lovely family and am now a teacher in a small school in Deadman's Creek, Illinois. I am very grateful to you, your friend Lily and all the other people who helped me on my journey.

I need your help or perhaps your guidance. I am very concerned about a young student. Her name is Alice Ackerman, and she's an orphan placed by the Orphan society. She doesn't say much but I believe she is being treated cruelly. She is thin to the point of starvation. She never brings lunch to school.

I tried speaking to her new, I hate to use the word, parents. I'm afraid I only made things worse for poor Alice.

I haven't seen any physical evidence of ill treatment, but I suspect she is being abused. She flinches when someone puts their hand on her arm or her back."

"My goodness, the poor child. We have to help

her, Kathleen." Lily stood up, pacing the floor trying to think.

"Lily sit down and let me finish the letter. We can't rush in. You know Father Nelson has already warned us the Orphan Society doesn't appreciate us taking over their cases."

"I don't care about them. If they did their jobs properly, we wouldn't have to interfere, would we?" Lily knew she was preaching to the converted, but she couldn't help it. Her blood boiled thinking of all the children sent to homes around the country who were in situations as bad or worse than this child. At least this young girl had a caring teacher. Someone was trying to look out for her. So many orphans were invisible. That made her mad.

"Lily, you can take that scowl off your face. We can only help the children if we keep calm and focus. Now let me finish the letter."

"Yes, mother!" Lily responded with a smile. Kathleen was right, as usual. Kathleen flashed her a quick smile before picking up the letter once more.

"I have expressed my concerns to the town council and the local Church but have been told to mind my business. The Ackermans have a long-standing reputation as law-abiding, churchgoing citizens.

To be frank, in this town the attitude to children from the orphan trains needs work. The general belief appears to be the children are from "evil" backgrounds and their "evilness" is contagious.

I would find myself another teaching position, but I can't bear to leave the children in my care. They need someone to show them a different viewpoint. Maybe I need to pray for humility, but I think God may have sent me here for a reason.

Miss Bridget, I love my job and don't want to have to give it up. But I remember your kindness to us on that train and I can't stand by and watch as a child is suffering. So, I write in hope there is some way you and your friends can help me and Alice. We believe she has family still living in New York.

I am not sure what I expect of you, but I have exhausted all other avenues. I wrote to the Orphans society to ask why they hadn't been to visit. I also made inquiries about Alice's background.

Alice doesn't remember much. She thinks her mother used to sing to her, but she doesn't recognize the language. It wasn't English. She said she was in the hospital for some time before she went to an orphanage where a Miss Baker worked. She has a rather nasty scar on the back of her head, covered by her hair thankfully as she is concerned enough about how she looks. She is a pretty young thing, but her new parents call her ugly. Alice has nightmares about rivers and boats."

Kathleen stopped reading to use her hanky. She blew her nose before wiping away the tears. Chills ran down the back of Lily's neck. This little girl, Alice, had already suffered so much. "Kathleen, what else does it say?"

Alice thinks her parents' names were Gustav and Agatha. Miss Baker told her, her mother died, but she didn't know what happened to her father. She remembers the name Haas which makes me think she may be from a German family. She has a doll with the letter A embroidered onto the dress. This might be for Alice.

Even as I write this letter, I pray for guidance in the hope I am doing the correct thing. Alice's situation will only get worse. She is nine years old and developing as a young woman. I can't bring myself to put my fears for her into words.

Miss Bridget, I don't know if you still work with children or if you will get this letter. I pray it will reach someone who can help us.

I wait in hope of a response.
Yours sincerely

Miss April Lawlor.

Kathleen glanced at Lily, "I wonder if Bridget remembers an April Lawlor. Do you?"

Lily shook her head. She couldn't remember any child called April but there had been so many over the years. It was possible Lawlor was her adoptive family name.

"What are we going to do, Kathleen? Do you agree it sounds like this child might be a survivor of the General Slocum? There aren't many children who fear boats and water and have German-sounding names."

"I agree but before we get too carried away, we need to check our options. A lot depends on whether these Ackerman people have formally adopted Alice. We need to speak to Charlie. He can find out what the legal position is to remove a child from the home, if the adoption is legal."

"He is due any minute. He said it was the only time he had time to speak to me without the children interrupting." Lily picked up a pen twiddling it in her fingers. "Frieda may know someone in Little Germany who can help us. I know the community isn't as close as it was, not since the tragedy but someone might remember."

"Good idea, Lily. She has a lot of contacts although I hate reminding her of that horrible day. But she sees Elsa all the time and we wouldn't have her if not for the tragedy."

Kathleen crossed herself, amusing Lily. Her friend had never lost her faith despite all the horrific things they had witnessed. Sometimes Lily envied Kathleen, would her thoughts be any more silent if she believed in a God who loved everyone?

Kathleen didn't seem to notice Lily's disquiet. "Father Nelson may help too."

"We will have to tread softly with him, Kathleen, he won't like us rocking the apple cart as he calls it. He's voiced his concerns about our interference with the Orphan Society before."

"He'll get over it when he hears a child is at risk." Kathleen retorted. "I know I told you to be calm, but I can't tell you how angry this letter makes me. How many people does one person have to tell before they listen? A child is suffering, and nobody will help this teacher. I feel like taking a trip to this town."

"Kathleen, what did you say about staying calm," Lily chided gently although she understood. She felt the same way. "We will rescue Alice from the Ackermans. I don't even know them, but I want to make sure they never have access to another child again."

"Who are you warring against now, my darling?" Charlie asked as he walked into the room. He kissed Kathleen on the cheek before pulling Lily into his arms and kissing her on the mouth.

"Charlie! What was that for?" Lily protested, smoothing her skirt with her hands.

"Can't I kiss my wife?" Charlie looked from one to the other. "What's wrong?"

Lily told him about the letter. "So, is there a way to get Alice back where she belongs?" she asked.

"We don't know where she belongs Lily. You would have to find her family in New York, assuming she has one." Charlie ran a hand through his graying hair. Only then did she notice how tired he looked.

"If Miss Lawlor can find proof of real neglect, she may get the sheriff to intervene."

"Charlie, the girl is starving. How much proof do we need?" Kathleen asked.

"I don't know Kathleen as I have never been to Illinois never mind know their laws. But from experience, it won't be easy unless we find a blood relative."

ORPHAN TRAIN STRIKE

Lily knew Charlie wasn't trying to be the voice of doom. He was just facing facts. Placing children in families was hard enough, getting them back again was something most people didn't even try to do.

She glanced at Kathleen recognizing the determination on her friend's face.

"Thanks Charlie. We will find her family. Kathleen, would you like to join us for lunch?"

"No but thank you. I'll write back to Miss Lawlor. Enjoy an hour away from our worries. They will still be here when you come back."

Lily kissed Kathleen on the cheek before leaving arm and arm with her husband. As they walked out the door to their favorite lunchtime spot, Charlie squeezed her fingers. "Darling, stop scowling. People will think I am forcing you to accompany me. Everything will be just fine, have faith."

Lily couldn't reply. She wasn't sure she had faith anymore. She plastered a smile on her face. Her husband deserved a nice lunch to take his mind off his own troubles. She put her arm through his. "They are just jealous I have such a lovely man to accompany me."

He chuckled and as always, his laugh cheered her up but this time it didn't still the negative voices in her head. Did Carmel's Mission and their work with the orphan train achieve anything or did they just provide a temporary solution? By shipping Alice and children like her to other areas in America, their aim to give the young a better future. But how many really benefited?

CHAPTER 20

OCTOBER 1909 NEW YORK

Maria stirred her coffee waiting for Frieda, who sometimes ran late at the hospital. She stared around the restaurant, making up stories about the other customers.

"Maria, I'm so sorry. Have you been waiting long?"

"Not really." Maria lied. She didn't want Frieda to feel worse.

"You look wonderful. Is that a new shirtwaist?"

Maria nodded. "Sewn by my own hand too. I've come a long way since I started working with Mrs. Stein."

"The Jewish lady who gave you the Lemon."

Maria nodded, her voice catching. Mrs. Stein didn't work in the factory anymore. A younger, less expensive worker had replaced her. Someone said the Steins had been evicted from their apartment and had gone to live with Mr. Stein's younger sister. It wasn't fair. Mrs. Stein had been a good and faithful employee but none of that mattered. All the owners seemed to care about was how much money they could make.

"Sorry Maria, I didn't mean to bring up bad memories."

"It's so unfair. The bosses can do what they like and we have to go along with it. Rosa says I should just get used to it but I can't. I want to scream from the rooftops how wrong it is." Maria noticed Frieda wasn't paying attention. "What's wrong with you?"

"Me? Sorry is it that obvious. Kathleen, Patrick's mother, has asked me to help locate the family of a little girl."

"And?"

"She's an orphan. They think her family died on the General Slocum."

"Frieda, no wonder you look upset. Hearing her story must bring up terrible memories."

"It does and I know I'm being selfish but I dread going to Little Germany. Every time, I go I see the faces who went that day and never came back. But this girl, Alice, needs help and I…"

"Need someone to go with you. How about right now?" Maria stood up. "I have a friend, Sarah. She's German but Jewish. I don't know if she can help but we will ask her. I know where she lives and it's close to here."

Frieda smiled. "Maria Mezza, when you put your mind to something, nothing changes it does it?"

"Are you calling me stubborn because there are some who'd say that cap fits you very well."

The girls giggled as they teased one another. Maria sent up a prayer of thanks, her Papa admired Frieda. Otherwise their friendship would have been more difficult.

"How is your father?"

"Better thank you. He still finds it a little difficult to breathe and spends a lot of time sitting but he says he is better."

"And Rosa?"

"Still in love. How she can bear to go out with Greco is beyond me. Papa's annoyed but she won't listen to him or Mama. She is besotted." Maria changed the subject.

"How's Patrick?"

Frieda's cheeks flushed. "Busy. He's

either working or studying. I rarely see him these days."

"Yet you go bright red at this name."

"Maria, stop teasing. Someday you will fall in love and then I will tease you."

"I don't have time for love. I need to find a new job and try to do my exams at night time. I haven't given up wanting to be a schoolteacher."

"Why don't you come and work at the Sanctuary? That would be perfect. You could sew in the mornings and teach some children in the evenings. Why don't I speak to Kathleen and Lily?"

"Frieda, stop please. You know I can't. I told Mama about Lily and the work she does a while ago. Rosa came in as I was speaking and she gave Mama a different version. You know about the women who once lived on the streets and stuff." Maria wished she hadn't started this conversation.

Frieda prompted, "What did your Mama say?"

"Not a lot but she went straight to mass and said a whole rosary. That's a lot of prayers."

"She doesn't approve of Lily?"

"It's not that exactly. She wasn't sure about us being friends." At Frieda's crestfallen face, Maria took her arm. "Stop worrying. Nothing could stop you being my friend. Sarah's home is at the top of this street."

"It's Saturday." Frieda protested. "We can't just arrive at her house."

"She isn't religious. She said to call anytime. She is dying to meet my doctor friend. Sarah believes in equality."

They called to the door and Sarah was pleased to see them. She listened as Frieda told her Alice's story. "I will ask my friends. There is a man called Gustav working at the Triangle. I don't know much about him. I can talk to him on Monday."

"Thank you, Sarah."

"How's old Reinhardt?" Sarah asked. "Does his breath still stink and is he still trying to get the young ones to work late alone?"

Maria shuddered. She could almost smell Reinhardt. "Yes and yes. I told him Mama would come to the factory to sit with me if I had to work late alone. You should have seen his face."

Sarah giggled. "I should have tried that one. I could have set my grandmother on him. She won't take any of his rubbish. She's gone to see Clara Lemlich at a meeting this evening. Father wouldn't let me go with her. Says Clara is just a rabble rouser."

"I think everyone underestimates Miss Lemlich because of her size. She is tiny, but she packs a punch. Do you think the factories will go out on strike?"

"Yes, Frieda, the women at the Triangle are fed up. I guess some of your lot will join in, Maria?"

Maria thought of Rosa. She wouldn't even listen to Maria griping about working conditions. "Some will. But I'm not sure of how many. Maybe the talks with the employers will work."

Sarah shrugged.

"You don't believe they will, do you Sarah?"

"No, Frieda, I don't. But we will see. Now why don't I introduce you to a few friends who may track your Alice's family?"

The girls spent a few hours in Little Germany. Frieda took them to meet Mrs. Sauer, the neighbor who'd looked after her when her family had died. She gave Mrs. Sauer the information she had about Alice. It wasn't a lot to go on, but the woman promised to do all she could.

"Don't let it be so long before you come back to see us, young Frieda."

"I won't."

Maria didn't comment. She could see the burden

on Frieda's shoulders as they left Little Germany behind them. She squeezed her friend's hand as a gesture of support. The whole time Sarah chatted away about the preparations being made for the strike.

Once they escorted Sarah home, they walked together back to Maria's house. Frieda said she would use the opportunity to check up on Maria's father.

"Evening, Miss Frieda. Are you here to measure me for my coffin?"

"Mr. Mezza, don't be saying things like that. You will damage my reputation." Frieda joked back.

Maria made the coffee marveling at the casual chatter between Frieda and her Papa.

"Maria told me you are not eating so well."

"Maria Mezza, some things are for family ears only!" Papa pretended to scold her.

"It is important you eat, Mr. Mezza otherwise you can't fight illness. You must try or I will come every night to feed you myself."

"A pretty face, that I can live with."

"Benito Mezza, I can hear you, you know. See what I have to put up. Married all these years and he flirts with a girl half my age. In my home."

Maria winked at Frieda who looked a little taken aback.

"Take no notice of my wife, Miss Frieda. She knows I haven't looked at another woman since I set eyes on her, a long time ago back home."

Frieda stood up. "I best get back. I have a lot of work to do. Think about what I said, Maria."

"What did you say? What has my Maria done now?"

"Nothing, Mr. Mezza."

Maria silently begged her friend to stay quiet but Frieda continued. "I suggested she consider a job at the Sanctuary. She can sew in the morning and in the afternoon teach the children. Lily and Kathleen would love to have someone like Maria working there."

Maria was afraid to look at either of her parents.

"She would earn more. The person in charge is a woman so no men like Reinhart to deal with."

Maria groaned. She hadn't mentioned her boss to Papa.

"All workers get a bowl of soup, bread and as much water as they want. No paying 2 cents for a cup of water."

Frieda flushed slightly. She seemed to realize

the change in the atmosphere and with a look at Maria, she stopped talking.

"Maria, you haven't said this place you work now is so awful."

Before Maria could answer her father, Mama spoke.

"Thank you for everything you do for my husband Miss Frieda. Maria is a good catholic girl. She will marry a nice boy. She must keep a good reputation."

Maria almost groaned aloud.

Frieda, flushed bright red now, stood up. Papa held out his hands. "Miss Frieda, you have a kind, generous heart. My Maria is lucky to have a friend like you."

Maria's eyes swam as she saw Frieda blink rapidly. She grabbed her coat.

"I will walk Frieda out." She didn't wait for permission but bustled her friend out of the apartment.

"Why didn't you listen to me earlier today?" she hissed as Frieda remained silent.

"I thought they might change their minds if they heard it from me. I didn't...I'm sorry." Frieda looked so unhappy, Maria's anger disappeared.

"Thank you for trying. Few care that much, Frieda. I am lucky we are friends."

Frieda smiled but her eyes looked suspiciously glassy. She insisted Maria go home. She would find a cab back to Carmel's mission.

* * *

The next morning, Frieda glanced up from her books. The exam was in a couple of weeks. She couldn't sleep the night before so concentrating was difficult. Yawning, she tried to make sense of the text, but it could have been written in ancient Greek. She looked up as someone knocked on her door.

"Come in," she called, closing over her textbook as Kathleen walked in. She noted her friend looked very tired.

"Frieda, I'm sorry to interrupt. I wanted to see if you would like to come for dinner this evening."

"No but thank you. I have to study."

"You look very tired, Frieda. Did you not sleep? Was it because of your visit to Little Germany?"

"No that went well. Here sit down. I'll take the bed. Maria came with me and a friend of hers, called Sarah. Sarah knows of someone called Gustav, he works at the Triangle. She will speak with him during the week."

Kathleen hugged her. "That's wonderful news. I will write to Miss Lawlor and give her an update. So why do you look so glum?"

"You know Maria wants to be a teacher, but she had to give up school due to Mr. Mezza being ill."

Kathleen nodded.

"I went to her house last night, he is fine but would be much better with a richer diet and nicer living quarters. I suggested Maria come and work here. She would earn more and could do some teaching with the little ones. I know she'd enjoy that."

Kathleen held her gaze making it difficult for Frieda to say what had happened next.

"I insulted the Mezza's. Mrs. Mezza said Maria was a good catholic girl and needed to be careful of her reputation."

"And this annoyed you?"

"Yes it did. We help people here not judge them. What does she think will happen to Maria? We'll sell her into slavery?"

"Frieda, don't be upset. Mrs. Mezza is protecting her daughter the best she can. New York is a huge and scary place to lots of immigrants. It's different from the life they knew back home. There they could keep their families safe. Here, well anything can happen. I'm sure they don't believe you are a fallen woman."

Frieda considered what Mr. Mezza had said.

"No, but… it would be so much better for Maria to work here."

"Yes, it might be but Maria isn't the type of girl we set the Sanctuary up for. Giving her a position could mean we couldn't help someone in a worse place."

Frieda put her hands to her mouth. "I didn't think of that."

"Frieda, your good nature makes you do things impulsively. Don't change. Sometimes things work out and other times it doesn't. But everything happens for a reason even if we don't always know that reason."

Kathleen stood up.

"I think you should take some time off and enjoy yourself. Come to the house for dinner. Elsa and Little Richie love to see you."

Frieda giggled. "Are you using blackmail?"

"Of course. If it works, don't knock it."

Frieda smiled but her eyes filled up.

"Please don't cry, Frieda."

"You and Richard, you helped me so much. Not just by paying for me to go to medical school but accepting me. Letting me visit with Elsa. You treat me as part of your family."

To her horror, Frieda watched as Kathleen wiped tears from her eyes.

"I couldn't be prouder of you than any real mother, Frieda. You follow your heart, regardless of the consequences. You remind me of Lily. I just want to protect you. I can't help it. I know you are an adult and can make you own choices, but I can't help feeling a little responsible for you. Does that make you angry?"

Frieda gulped back the tears. "No. It makes me feel… wanted."

"You are very much wanted." Kathleen put her arms out and gave Frieda a hug. "Now open your books and study hard young woman. I expect you to ace those exams." Kathleen stood up.

Frieda nodded. As soon as the door closed behind Kathleen, she opened the book and began studying with a vengeance. Double Greek or not, this text would not beat her. She had exams to pass.

CHAPTER 21

NOVEMBER 1909

"Maria. What's taking you so long? The bell rang five minutes ago." Maria jumped as Rosa laid her hand on her arm. All around her, her co-workers were standing, stretching and talking all at once. It was the end of another busy day.

"Sorry Rosa, I was thinking about Papa."

"I don't want to talk about Papa. Don't forget to tell Mama, I came with you and your friend tonight for a walk. I will be home later."

"Where are you going?" Maria asked her older sister, but it was pointless. Rosa was still walking out with Paulo, her parents didn't approve of him as he was a member of the Mafia. Maria didn't care about that, she didn't like Paulo as he was a bully.

She'd heard stories of him beating up other men and being involved in fights. She also heard he liked the ladies, a lot! But her sister thought he was wonderful. It was Paulo this and Paulo that.

"Be careful Rosa. You know his reputation."

"I can handle myself," Rosa retorted, twisting her hair back into a neater style. "Paulo loves me and in time you will see me wearing his ring."

Not if Papa had anything to say about it, she wouldn't. Maria didn't put her thoughts into words. Rosa was headstrong and only got more stubborn if anyone argued with her. It was best to let her sister think she had Maria's support. She hoped with time, Rosa would see Paulo for what he was before she did anything stupid.

Rosa turned and pinched Maria on the arm, getting her attention.

"What was that for?" Maria rubbed the sore patch on her arm.

"You are not to go to any strike meetings. Word travels fast and the bosses won't like it."

"I don't care what they like," Maria retorted pulling her arm out of Rosa's reach. "What I do in my time is my business."

"You should care. They hold all the power and if

you think those stupid girls can change anything, you are sillier than you look. Paulo says it's only a matter of time before the factory owners get serious and blacklist anyone who even thinks of the word strike."

Maria's heart slowed as her sister put her worst fears into words.

"What do you mean when they get serious? What does Paulo call beating up Clara Lemlich? You know the young Jewish girl with the beautiful voice. She was picketing peacefully when those thugs hired by the factory owners beat her up. They broke several of her ribs. Not that it stopped her, she works harder than before."

Rosa didn't say a word causing Maria to lose hold of her temper. "Rosa, listen to me. You can fool yourself all you want but don't pretend he knows nothing about it. The Mafia knows everything, more than the police and probably just as much as the gangsters involved. Maybe they were even Mafiosi."

Rosa paled, clutching Maria's arm.

"Don't joke Maria," Rosa hissed. "Not like that. Anyone could hear you." Rosa looked around her. Maria didn't think anyone was paying them any attention. The Mezza girls had a reputation for fighting with each other. It was normal for Italian siblings especially the girls.

"Maria, stay away from Clara and her friends. That way only leads to tears. What you need is to find a nice Italian boy and think about settling down." Rosa put a scarf over her hair, taking care not to mess up the new style.

"What like Paulo? No, thank you." Maria regretted being so short as soon as the words were out of her mouth. Rosa was only trying to look out for her. She saw anger flare in her sister's expression. "Rosa, I'm sorry."

"Save it. What do I care anyway?" Rosa stormed out.

Maria put away the materials on her desk. She hated her workspace being untidy. As she made her way downstairs, she passed some cutters. All men, they were a law unto themselves. The no smoking policy in the factory didn't seem to apply to them. Still, they were a nice enough bunch so long as you treated them with the respect, they thought they deserved.

"Ciao, Bella," some said while others whistled as she walked by, but she just smiled back. It didn't do to get on their wrong side. The best cutters could name their price and the factory owners knew it.

* * *

MARIA STARED at the thousands of men and women standing around her. Even on the stage, there was barely enough room for all the speakers. She held hands with Frieda, terrified the crush of people would separate them. Maria had never liked crowds, but this was important.

"That's Mary Dreier, she's the president of the Women's Trade Union League."

Maria remembered reading something about the woman in the paper. She protested against lockout, when the factory owners replaced their striking workers with newly hired girls.

"She's the rich lady arrested outside the Triangle shirtwaist factory when she joined the strikers, isn't she?"

"Yes, Maria, the papers helped us a lot when they printed the story. I bet the policeman who arrested her is sorry he did."

"I don't have any sympathy for him. He shouldn't have arrested her when he knew she was innocent. She didn't hit that strike breaker. Everyone knew the girl was lying." Maria didn't hide her disgust. She could understand some people had to work through the strike. They couldn't afford to be without an income, but it was one thing walking past your friends but another to lie about one of them hitting you.

Maria clutched Frieda's arm as the crowd surged. Short of standing on the ceiling, there was literally no room for anyone else. The atmosphere was amazing with people clapping, shouting and stamping their feet. She couldn't hear the speakers but that didn't matter. She got the general gist of what they were saying. Then the room fell silent.

"Who's that woman with her?" Maria asked Frieda.

"It's Clara Lemlich," Frieda shouted into Maria's ear. Maria stared at this woman who'd she heard some much about. Rumor had it, her family had immigrated to the USA after a pogrom in their local village back in the Ukraine. Why was there so much hatred in the world? Maria studied Clara. How could a slightly built young woman have such a strong voice? Maria moved forward eager to hear her words even if she didn't understand Yiddish. Clara held up her hands for silence. Then she spoke. Frieda whispered the translation to Maria.

"We must take action. The time for talking has passed. This is our best chance to get the deal we want. The life we want not just for ourselves and

ORPHAN TRAIN STRIKE

our coworkers but for future generations of men and women living in or arriving in this amazing country."

Maria cheered with the rest. She believed every word Clara said. They were striking not just for better pay and working conditions but for the right to have a life outside the factory.

The crowd roared their approval when Clara said the strike would go ahead the next day. At a set time, all the workers would walk out together in unity. The factory owners would have no choice but to listen.

The cheering, waving of hats and clapping of hands went on for at least five minutes. Maria and Frieda exchanged a grin. This was it. They were living through one of the most exciting periods on earth.

The crowd poured out of the meeting hall and into the streets outside, everyone talking at once.

"Even Rosa will have to listen now. Times are changing," Maria gushed.

"Clara is wonderful, isn't she? So brave, so fierce. I can't imagine any factory owner not giving her what she wants. Can you?" Frieda asked.

CHAPTER 22

Maria walked home on a high. Her mama and papa had, to her surprise, agreed with the strike. Mama took some convincing, but Papa said if things didn't change, more would die. The conditions in the factories were worse than the sweatshops in the tenements and that said a lot. Papa told her to stick with her conscience. She teared up as she remembered him having to breathe heavily, trying to get the words out. She'd hugged him close, feeling his bones through his shirt. His condition scared her, but he insisted he was feeling better. He said it was important they take a stand so that the future generations didn't suffer like he and workers like him had done.

Thrown onto a scrap heap and forgotten about as soon as his usefulness to his employer ended.

* * *

THE NEXT MORNING Maria and her fellow shirtwaist workers sat around their machines. The air was full of tension. She knew some of her coworkers had been at the meeting and taken the vow to strike but how many of the others would down tools and follow them. She pushed her bag and coat under her feet, ready to move when the time came. Rosa stared at her, her mouth a tight line. Paulo had forbidden Rosa to join the strike. His opinion meant more to her sister than that of their parents.

Then there was a shout, and everyone stopped working, picked up their coats and walked out of the factory together. Maria made her way down the stairs, her body shaking with excitement and a little fear. She had taken the first step to a better future. She wished Rosa was beside her, but her sister had made her way toward the restroom. Maybe she would reconsider when she saw the number of empty desks.

She gasped as the cold wind hit her, pulling her coat tighter around her. Her fellow workers fell silent and Maria soon saw why. A row of police, batons drawn were waiting for them. She refused to acknowledge their presence and instead turned on her heel and followed the leader towards the nearby meeting hall. Leaders of the local 25 were waiting for them. The leaders asked those who could read and write to put their terms on paper.

She sucked the end of her pencil as she looked at what she'd written:

1) Committee to arrange wages not someone like Reinhardt.

2) Advance notice of busy periods so they could plan childcare etc.

3) Set working hours

That was it wasn't it? No, she was missing something. Her mother's face popped into her head.

4) Sunday was a day of rest.

Maria grinned at another striker as she handed in the papers and walked outside to wait for Frieda.

"There you are. Sorry I'm late. I had to get a job finished for Lily." Frieda explained before she introduced some women with her. They were all from Carmel's mission.

Maria stared at Frieda. "What are your friends

doing here? They don't need to strike, not with their working conditions."

Frieda put her arm through Maria's, shivering despite her thick woolen coat.

"I know but Lily wants us to show our support. She arranged for me to have some time off from the hospital, told Dr. Green my medical skills might prove useful."

Maria took a deep breath at which Frieda immediately rushed to reassure her. "Sorry Maria don't worry. She doesn't really think trouble will break out. She and Kathleen will be along sometime later today. Which picket line are we joining?"

Maria didn't know. Frieda asked one of the Local 25 and soon they joined a group of young women outside one of the smaller factory buildings. They walked up and down to keep warm.

"So did Rosa join us?" Frieda asked, blowing on her hands.

"I don't know. The last I saw of her, she was heading to the ladies room. Paulo, her boyfriend, doesn't agree with the strike."

"What does Rosa think?"

"Frieda, I think she has forgotten how." Maria stopped, she didn't enjoy being mean, but Frieda was her friend and she knew Rosa. "All we hear now is what Paulo thinks. I don't understand what she sees in him. I'm sure Papa shed a tear when she announced she was engaged. Paulo should have asked Papa." Maria paused, aware Frieda was an orphan. "Sorry, I let my mouth run away with me."

"Don't be. It would be the same with me if Vati was alive. It is not respectful if the man doesn't ask the girl's father."

"Paulo doesn't care, and Papa can't do anything. Not in his state but even if he wasn't ill, he would have to be careful. The Mafia... it has power." Maria didn't want to think about what she had heard about the gang both here and back in Sicily.

Frieda squeezed her hand in a gesture of support. They walked in silence for a while.

"Did you see Sarah? Has she any news of Alice's family?"

"Sorry, Frieda, she hasn't had a chance to check. The Triangle bosses fired Sarah when they found out she was in the Union. They warned her, the police will arrest her if she goes near the Triangle building."

"That's not right or fair. This is America. She's free to go where she wants."

Alice shrugged. "Sarah doesn't want to risk it. She said she will try to find out where Gustav lives and speak to him at home."

"I hope she finds him. It would be a lovely Christmas gift for Alice to find her father."

CHAPTER 23

"Alice, can you stay back after school, please? I'd like to discuss something with you."

"Yes, Miss Lawlor." Her heart beat faster. What did the teacher want? She studied her face but couldn't read anything into it. She didn't appear annoyed.

When the bell came at the end of class, Jack whispered.

"I'll wait for you outside and walk you home."

Alice nodded, feeling sick. She cleaned the board and straightened the desks while Miss Lawlor said goodbye to her pupils.

"Thank you Alice. Why don't you take a seat?"

"Are you leaving?" Alice burst out.

"No. It's not bad news but I also don't want you to get your hopes up, Alice. What I have to say, I'd like to stay between you and me. It's important. Do you understand?"

She nodded, watching as Miss Lawlor took a letter out of her pocket.

"I wrote to an old friend in New York. She looked after me when I traveled the orphan train. Her sister responded. Alice, I told them about you."

Vomit rose in her throat, her head spinning.

"You promised not to…"

"I know I promised, but it was one I couldn't keep. Alice, I care about you. I hate the fact you are starving and being beaten. Don't deny it."

Alice stared at her feet. Didn't Miss Lawlor understand she would only make things worse?

"Kathleen Green, she wrote me back. She has friends from a place called Little Germany in New York. Have you heard of it?"

Alice shook her head, too miserable to work out why her teacher was torturing her.

"I think you may have once lived there."

Alice couldn't breathe.

"With your parents. Alice, do you know about the General Slocum disaster?"

Alice couldn't answer, her heart hammered against her chest, her hands clammy.

"It was the name of a ship that sank in New York. There was a group of people on board, a church picnic. Lots of women and children, some family groups but a lot of the men had to stay home to go to work. There was a fire on the boat and…"

The fire on the water. She hadn't imagined it. Tears sprung into her eyes.

"The water was on fire. I could feel it," she whispered.

"Alice, I think you were on that boat with your mother. I don't know if your father was there too. I've asked my friends to find out more."

"You think my father might be alive?"

Miss Lawlor put her hand under Alice's chin.

"Look at me, Alice. This is very important. I don't know if you have a family but I won't rest until I find out. I debated whether to tell you. I didn't want to hurt you." Miss Lawlor look a deep breathe before saying, "I believe we all need hope in our lives and friends. I want to give you both."

"I have friends. Jack and Jacob. Wolf."

"I hope we are friends, Alice. Can you understand why it's important you don't say a word to anyone not even the twins? We don't want the wrong people to hear about my letters."

She meant the Ackermans. They would stop Alice from finding anyone.

"I won't tell anyone." Alice crossed her heart. "But when will you know? Tomorrow?"

Miss Lawlor rubbed her finger against Alice's cheek. "It may take a long time. Many people died, and those who lived, well they moved away. They couldn't face the sadness."

Alice thought about that for a few minutes. "But what if my father doesn't want me? He sent me away. He must have or I wouldn't be here."

A shadow crossed the teacher's face before she tried to smile.

"Maybe your father's injuries prevented him from claiming you. Or there could be other reasons. Let's just have a little more patience and see."

Alice gulped hard, she didn't want to cry but what if her father didn't want her? What if Miss Lawlor found him and he said no?

"Don't look so glum, Alice. Have faith. I wish I could cuddle you but I don't want to hurt you."

Alice's back was raw from another beating. She

leaned in to kiss Miss Lawlor on the cheek, feeling her tears.

"Thank you for caring."

Alice couldn't say anymore. The tears fell down Miss Lawlor's cheeks and her shoulders were shaking. Alice ran out of the classroom and down the street completely forgetting Jack was waiting for her.

"Alice, wait up. What's wrong?"

"Nothing. I got to get home. I can't be late. See you tomorrow."

She hoped Jack would take the hint. She needed to be alone.

Eliza wasn't home to question her. Alice raced through her chores and then went to the barn to be with Wolf. She sobbed as she told the dog what had happened.

"What if he doesn't want me? What if he's mad when they find him?"

Wolf licked her tears but nothing could make her feel better.

For the next week, she asked Miss Lawlor every day had a letter arrived. Then she asked every couple of days until she gave up. Either they hadn't found her family, or they had and they didn't want her either.

She gave up trying to keep Eliza and him happy. She did what they expected without speaking. He was away more than ever. When he came home, all he could rant about was some strike in New York. Alice had asked Miss Lawlor about it. She said some women were marching in the streets of New York because of their horrible working conditions. Alice didn't know what that had to do with him.

She woke to the sound of an argument.

"Women cause all my problems. Those immigrants in New York who should be grateful to America for taking them in are bad enough. Their strikes are taking food from our mouths and money from our wallets. But you don't care do you? You keep spending money like it was growing on the trees."

Alice crept down the stairs and sat on the last step. She didn't want to walk in on the argument but she didn't want to be in trouble for being late for breakfast either. Not when he was all riled up.

"Ned, it was only two dollars. You needed a new shirt, your old one is all frayed."

"You stupid woman, can you hear yourself? Only two dollars. Do you know how hard I have to work to earn that money?"

Alice flinched as she heard the slap quickly followed by a second.

"Ned, stop it. You're hurting me."

"Don't you tell me what to do in my home."

The sound of plates crashing brought Alice running. She couldn't stand by and let him hurt someone else.

"Stop it."

Her shout seemed to bring him to his senses.

"Another useless girl. Heaven help me that's all I need."

He grabbed his hat and stormed out the door, slamming it behind him. Alice put her hand out to Eliza but got pushed aside. Blood poured from a cut above her eye and she held her side.

"Want me to get the doctor?"

Eliza shook her head.

Alice filled a bowl with cold water, wet a clean cloth using it to staunch the flow of blood from the cut. She made her mother a cup of tea. Eliza gulped it.

"You best get to school. Not a word to anyone, do you hear?"

"Do you want me to stay home with you?"

"No!" Eliza shouted but the pain must have

been bad as she swayed in the seat. Alice hovered not sure what to do. Eliza whispered,

"Thank you Alice. I'll be fine. Go on, get to school. Take a muffin with you."

Shocked at Eliza's niceness, Alice hesitated but only for a second. She grabbed the muffin and left. He might come back and she didn't want him starting on her.

She was late arriving at school. Miss Lawlor gave her a concerned look but Alice shook her head. "I'm fine. Mother hit her head. I helped her clean up."

Miss Lawlor raised her eyebrows, but Alice refused to say anything more. Later, at question time, a time when the children could ask any question they wanted, Alice put her hand up.

"Miss Lawlor, when will the strike in New York be over?"

"Good question, Alice. I don't know. The women are fighting hard for what they believe in. Many are separated from their families and jailed. One wonders how long they can hold out?"

CHAPTER 24

Frieda hugged her sides as she sat in the cell, trying to keep warm. She'd given her coat to one of the youngest strikers. Lily and the other ladies at the sanctuary would be frantic. Would they be angry too? She had only meant to lend support not get herself arrested. It had all happened so quickly. One minute she was talking to two Jewish seamstresses about how the strike was impacting their home life, the next minute she was fighting a policeman. He'd used his truncheon to club a poor girl half his size. The police were there to protect the citizens. In the strike, they were on the side of the factory owners and not the women on the picket lines.

"Sir, stop it, now." Frieda stood up to the policeman, but his answer was to hit her across the shoulder. She fell to the ground. He dragged her up and put her in the back of the wagon. Half dazed, she found herself in a holding cell surrounded by other strikers and four or five drunk women. Judging by their clothes, they were ladies of the night.

"What's a girl like you doing in here?"

Frieda glanced at the women, recognizing her. "Susie, it's me Frieda from the sanctuary. Are you all right? Your arm is bleeding?"

"That's nothing. What did you do?" Eyes alight with curiosity, Susie moved closer. The combination of sweat, drink and other unknown scents made Frieda retch, but she masked her reaction.

"I didn't do anything wrong, Susie. I was talking to two of the strikers. Lily asked me to check on them and next thing I am in here. They arrested me for assaulting a police officer. Only he assaulted me."

Susie nodded, "We keep hearing the same thing. Shocking it is. The coppers are used to beating women like me but to hit young innocent girls, it's just wrong."

"Susie, they shouldn't hit anyone."

Susie didn't argue. Frieda saw the woman believed women like her deserved it and worse. That attitude incensed Frieda. Susie interrupted her thoughts.

"Why don't the women go back to work, Frieda? They ain't going to achieve nothing, picketing like they are. Nobody cares. They got jobs don't they and families to feed. Its nearly Christmas. The weather ain't too bad but it will be cold come New Year."

Poor Susie, she couldn't believe those working indoors could have it almost as bad as the life she lived on the streets.

"I know but they can't go back. Not until the bosses agree to the union terms otherwise, it will be all for nothing."

"But what do they want? I can't understand it myself. Wouldn't mind a job indoors. Might be better than what I have to do."

Frieda couldn't argue with that. She understood why Susie found it hard to have pity for the strikers, but she didn't have a clue how bad things were for them.

"Susie, I know life is hard for you. But these women have it bad too. They work fourteen hours a day for a pittance. There're young children working in places they shouldn't be. Many die or suffer severe injuries. They have to work Saturday and Sundays too if the boss says so. It's no life."

Susie shrugged her shoulders, wrapping the moth-eaten wrap closer around herself.

"Aye I suppose they have their troubles, but they are only making life worse. Women will never beat the men of this city. They be too powerful."

Frieda opened her mouth, but Susie beat her to it. "See that girl over there. Raped by her employer and she is only a fourteen-year-old. The Judge fined her ten dollars. Where in God's name is, she supposed to get that money? Off to the workhouse she goes. Believe me, she'll be working the streets in a few years' time. Wouldn't surprise me if she ended up on Lily's doorstep."

Frieda knew Susie's background involved a similar assault. She didn't know how to comfort the woman.

Leonie, one girl she knew from Little Germany cried out as a streetwalker tried to grab her coat. Susie attacked the woman while Frieda pulled Leonie clear. "I couldn't let her have your coat. You were so kind to give it to me."

"Keep the coat, Leonie. I will talk to Lily about what we can do for your family so try not to worry."

"Since Papa left, it's been hard but now it's much worse. Mama's accident means she can't work. She worked for that company for five years and got nothing even though it was their fault. The little ones are always hungry and don't have proper shoes. When will it get better, Frieda?"

"I don't know," Frieda held Leonie as the girl sobbed. Then she pulled her into a seating position on the floor. "I have a friend looking for someone who we think lived in Little Germany. Alice, she's nine years old, thinks she lived there with her father called Gustav and her mother. Do you know of the family?"

Leonie shook her head. "Mutti might. She knows many people. I'll ask her when I get home."

Frieda let the younger girl sleep on her shoulder. She could feel her bones through her clothes. Her anger kept her awake. The cell was full of human misery, much of it preventable. When would the powers in New York listen?

Frieda heard her name being called along with thirteen other strikers. They filed into the courtroom. Frieda glanced at the judge, practicing the words she'd use to plead their case. She didn't have time to say anything. He fined them all ten dollars except for those strikers with arrest records. They got fined twenty-five dollars. Frieda couldn't believe her ears. How were the women going to pay those fees? It would be the workhouse. Then what would happen to their families?

"Frieda, I must break the strike. I don't want to be a scab, but I can't fight it anymore. Mutti sits in that dark, cheerless room on her own for hours. We don't have the money to light a fire, I barely find enough to give her a cup of tea and some old bread. How will I find ten dollars? It's over. I have to go back to work. I just have to."

"Leonie, don't cry. We will find a way. I'll talk to Lily. There has to be more we can do. Why don't you come back to the sanctuary with me now?"

"I can't. I've got to get home to Mutti. She'll be out of her head with worry."

Frieda watched Leonie stroll down the street, her shoulders weighed down with the weight of her worries. That was no life for a child. Sighing, she turned in the sanctuary's direction. She had no money for a cab now so would have to walk. She talked to herself the whole way home. It helped keep her distracted from who or what might lurk in the dark street corners.

* * *

Relieved beyond measure to reach the Sanctuary unharmed, she turned her key in the door only to have it pulled open.

"Frieda, oh my goodness I was so worried." Lily greeted her before dragging her into the sitting room where a small fire was still alight.

Frieda moved closer, hoping to take the chill from her bones.

"Lily, what are you doing here? You should be at home with your family."

"I couldn't go home, not while you were still out there What happened, where were you?" Lily asked, standing over her.

"I was in jail."

Lily sat with a bump. "What?"

"They arrested me for assaulting a police officer. I didn't touch him, Lily I swear. He hit me but then I got arrested. It was horrible. The cells were full of women. I met Susie, and she said…."

"Slow down Frieda." Lily stood up again and

hugged her close. "You're frozen. Where's your coat?"

"I gave it to Leonie, she didn't have one."

"Let's go to the kitchen. You need something to eat and we both need a cup of tea. Then tell me the story. Slowly, my mind is not working as it should."

Lily made the tea as Frieda ate some bread and cold meat. While eating, she told Lily the events of the night before. Lily's harsh intake of breath was the only reaction to the story of the fourteen-year-old rape victim. When Frieda finished her story, the silence lingered. Frieda kept eating giving Lily time to put her thoughts in order. She knew Lily well enough to know she was trying to put a plan together on how best they could help.

"You are right, Frieda. We have to do something. First, we need to clear those fines. Those women have enough to worry about. Leonie's mother, we will ask Richard Green to check on her. Or Patrick."

Frieda glanced away at the mention of his name. She hoped Lily couldn't see her flushed cheeks.

"Then we have to get more money into the hands of the strikers. Or maybe not money, but food baskets and clothes. Coats and gloves although thank goodness the snow hasn't come yet. For winter we are doing well with the weather apart from the rain."

Frieda tried to keep her eyes open as Lily came up with different things they needed to do. All she wanted was her bed. She had to sleep.

"We need to raise more money. Tonight will be a good start. Frieda, I found you a beautiful dress. It will go wonderfully with your hair. Bring out the green of your eyes too. You will stun the audience and make them open their wallets."

Tonight! Frieda groaned. She had completely forgotten about it. It was too much. What did she care about dresses when Leonie, Susie and others needed her?

"What's wrong? You'll not back out, will you? I know you are tired but your voice needs to be heard. Only you can tell the story of what it is really like on the picket lines. You can convince these rich women to help us help Leonie and her friends."

"Yes, Lily, I won't let you down." Frieda would do anything for this woman and Kathleen who had both, in their own way, helped her so much. She was bone tired and had studying to catch up on, but it would have to wait. It was only one night. Two hours if she went, did her talk and then came home early.

"Good girl, go on up to bed. I will tell the other ladies to let you sleep today. I will drop a note to Inspector Griffin too to tell him about the police's disgraceful behavior last night. He may do something."

"I doubt it, Lily."

Lily held her gaze. "Why? Is there something you haven't told me?"

"I didn't know for certain until last night." Frieda's cheeks flushed. She didn't want this wonderful woman to think she had done anything deceitful. "I was talking to some ladies back in Little Germany and also to the strikers. I thought it unusual the police were being so heavy-handed. It turns out they believe the owners of certain factories have paid bribes for the police to look the other way. Like they paid those men to beat up Clara. They have arrested no one for her assault."

Lily's mouth thinned. "Some of those shirtwaist factory owners think they are above the law. They aren't. Nobody is. I will call to see Inspector Griffin instead of writing. These bully boy tactics have to stop. He will know who I need to speak to."

Frieda couldn't help but feel a little sorry for

Inspector Griffin. He was a kind man and would never countenance police brutality. But he was only one man in the police force. Still, there was no point in trying to dissuade Lily. When she got it into her head to do something, nothing could stop her.

"Lily, I almost forgot. Leonie will ask her mother about Alice."

Lily's face darkened. "Father Nelson was here yesterday. He admitted he had written to the Orphan Society demanding someone go check on Alice."

"Why is that a bad thing?"

"I have a bad feeling, Frieda. Miss Lawlor wrote to say the Ackerman's hadn't appreciated her asking questions. What will they do when the Orphan Society arrive?"

Frieda yawned, putting a hand up to her face, muttering an apology.

"Off to bed with you now Frieda. We can't do anything about Alice at the moment. We can help the strikers. Patrick will collect you this evening. Kathleen and I have some business to attend to. We shall meet you there."

Frieda didn't look up. She would see Patrick later. What would he think of her all dressed up? Would she look like a woman or would he still see her as the child from Little Germany?

She ended up going alone to the function, meeting Kathleen and Lily there. Patrick had an emergency at the hospital. Disappointed, she couldn't really complain. The needs of the patient had to come first.

CHAPTER 25

*E*liza called for Alice to come downstairs. Heart hammering, she walked as slowly as she could. Christmas was approaching, the worst time of the year with the Ackermans becoming vicious.

Eliza didn't use the strap to hit her, but her hand stung just the same. Alice pushed the door to the front room open. There were two strangers sitting on the sofa. One a stern looking older woman with glasses and graying hair tied up in a severe bun. The other a younger woman dressed in a shirtwaist and a skirt that was a little too tight. Perhaps that's why she was red faced. The women looked out of place in the small fussy room.

The ladies looked anything but comfortable. She knew the sofa was all lumpy and spiky.

The whole room lacked brightness. The brown rug on the floor although brown highlighted the mud the ladies must have walked in. Alice sighed, it would fall to her to clean both the rug, and the matching colored floorboards underneath. She caught one woman looking at the empty grate. Eliza stood up as Alice walked toward her.

"There you are my dear. Mrs. Weiss and Miss Castle called to see us, aren't they kind?"

Alice nodded, not sure what to say. Eliza came over to her and placing a hand on her shoulder, spoke to the ladies.

"I was so lucky when little Alice stepped off that train. I prayed for a daughter and God was good. That was almost three years ago now. She isn't much to look at, but she has a good heart."

Alice had to stop her mouth from falling open. Why was Eliza being so nice? She stared at the two women. The younger one, Miss Castle had some paperwork in her hand. She tried not to wince as Eliza's grip tightened on her shoulder.

"Alice sweetheart, these ladies are from the Orphan's charity. They came to check on you.

Seems someone told them, I can't put such a thing into words it is just too shocking."

Alice stared in astonishment as tears fell from Eliza's eyes. She had never seen the woman show any emotion let alone cry. Why were these women here? What had Miss Lawlor done? She'd promised not to say anything to the Ackermans. This was worse. Eliza would blame her. He'd kill her.

"I wish my husband was here. You should see what a great father he is. Alice just adores him, don't you darling?"

Alice jumped as Eliza pinched her. She hadn't stayed dumb on purpose, but this was all so strange she didn't know how to act. She didn't have time to answer as the younger woman spoke. She had a nice soft voice.

"Alice, my name is Miss Castle. I work for the Orphans society. We wanted to see how you were. Do you enjoy your life here with the Ackermans?"

Alice looked from Miss Castle who had kind eyes to the woman beside her. Mrs. Weiss glared at Alice giving her the impression the older woman could read her thoughts. Should she tell the truth? If she told these women about the beatings and starvation would they take her back to her family?

"Tell the nice ladies, Alice."

Alice looked at Eliza. There was no mistaking the threat in Eliza's eyes. That look promised, tell them the truth and you will pay the price. She glanced again at the visitors, should she? Could she?

"Is the child mentally disturbed?" Mrs. Weiss asked, her gaze raking over Alice.

"Please don't speak harshly about my Alice," Eliza rebuked the visitor. "She gets nervous in front of strangers, don't you darling?"

"Yes, Mother." Alice stuck with Eliza, she was the safest bet. At least she knew where she stood with her "mother".

"Do you get enough to eat, Alice? You look rather thin for your age." Miss Castle spoke, her eyes seeming to plead with Alice to tell the truth. But Alice saw Mrs. Weiss wasn't interested in her and even less interested in the truth. She didn't answer, she wasn't about to lie not if she could avoid it.

"Miss Castle asked you a question, Alice."

"Sorry Mother. Yes, Miss Castle, Mother gives me plenty of food, but I don't eat much. Mother goes to great effort to find foods I like to eat." Alice spat out the words, her fingers crossed in the hope God wouldn't hold the lies against her.

Eliza hugged her close. Alice restrained the urge to pull away. She forced herself not to gag at the smell.

"She is having a growth spurt at the moment. You should have seen the state of her when she first arrived. All arms and legs. But now she is filling out nicely for a young lady. Nobody wants their child looking like a Thanksgiving turkey, do they?"

Alice winced at Eliza's horrible remark. She knew her mother was calling the younger woman fat. She wanted to tell Miss Castle to ignore Eliza's comment, but it was too late as she heard the younger woman sniff. But it was Mrs. Weiss who proved her instincts not to trust the woman was right.

"Quite right Mrs. Ackerman. Far too many women walking around who would benefit from some cleaner living. Isn't that right Penelope?"

Miss Castle looked at the ground but stayed silent.

Mrs. Weiss stood up. "We have taken up enough of your time. Please forgive us for descending on you like this but we must take seriously all complaints. You understand?" Mrs. Weiss didn't expect an answer as she headed toward the door.

"Yes." Eliza practically drooled over the older woman. "Let me walk you out. Alice stay here, please. It's cold outside and we don't want you getting a chill. So, Mrs. Weiss, can you tell me who made the complaint?"

"That is privileged information,"Miss Castle said. At a withering look from Mrs. Weiss she stopped talking. Mrs. Weiss whispered with Eliza as they walked together to the front door. Alice did as she had been told and stayed behind. It wouldn't do any good though as Eliza would blame her for whoever had complained.

Miss Castle moved closer to her and whispered,

"Alice, please remember we are here to protect you. If you ever need help, get someone to write to us. This is our address." Miss Castle shoved a card into Alice's hand before moving as fast as she could to follow the other women. Alice held the card in wonder. They were based in New York.

She knew she should stay where she was, but the temptation was too much. "Miss Castle wait please. Do you know anything about my father?"

The woman glanced toward her companion and Eliza before stepping back into the house.

"Nothing other than what you have been told. His name, Gustav Weber and an old address but nobody lives there anymore. Sorry Alice, it's not too helpful. I only briefly looked at your file. I best go, Mrs. Weiss is waiting."

Alice didn't follow. Eliza had already spotted her and from the expression in her eyes, Alice knew she was in big trouble. Eliza would wait until the ladies left. Miss Castle seemed to find it difficult to get into the wagon. Mrs. Weiss was talking loudly to her.

Alice turned away from the door looking for a hiding place for Miss Castle's card. She needed to memorize the address but there wasn't time now. She slid it into the middle of a book on the bookcase near the front door. Nobody ever read these books, they were for show only. The card was safe. Safer than her if Eliza's thunderous expression was anything to go by.

She didn't have to wait long. The ladies had barely pulled out of the gates when Eliza came back into the house and slammed the front door. "I suppose you put the teacher up to it. Don't deny it. It's written all over your face. Go to bed, Alice. Your father will deal with this when he gets back.

Until that time comes, I don't want to see your face. Do you hear me?"

"But he's not due back until Saturday. It's school tomorrow. We are…"

"You are never going back to school. I knew that woman was trouble from the minute she arrived with her modern ways. How dare she file a complaint about us? What have you been telling her, you ungrateful wretch?" Eliza's face turned purple as her voice rose. Wolf growled from the far side of the door.

Alice grabbed her chance as his noise distracted Eliza. She pulled the door and opened it, all set to run away. She couldn't bear it anymore. She didn't count on Eliza putting her foot out, tripping Alice headlong into the porch. She tumbled down the front steps and ended up sprawled out on the dirt. Wolf growled but kept his distance. He would have stayed like that, but Eliza's temper got the better of her. Alice saw her adoptive mother grab something and hit her across the shoulders. The agonizing pain brought tears to her eyes. She screamed as Eliza hit her again and again. Wolf jumped, snarling, his fangs visible. Alice heard a scream quickly muffled before she passed out.

Sniffing in her ear brought her round. Wolf

was pawing at her and whimpering. He kept pushing at her head until she lifted it. The pain, she grabbed the back of her scalp and her hand came away covered in blood. Wolf licked her face, alternatively licking and whimpering.

"I'm fine boy. Where is she?"

Wolf kept licking her and pushing her with his head. He was trying to get her to stand up, but her legs weren't responding. She dragged herself to a sitting position, the world spinning as the trees, sky and ground blended together. Blinking rapidly, her vision cleared enough for her to look toward the house. Eliza lay in the doorway to the house. She wasn't moving. Alice tried to move toward the house, but Wolf growled as she did so. He latched onto her dress and tried to pull her.

"Where do you want to go? We have to help her."

He growled and ran down the garden before coming back to Alice. He pawed at the ground, barking and running around. He was trying to warn her. Eliza didn't seem like she could hurt her. But what if Eliza woke up? Alice's clothes were filthy not only covered in dirt but in blood and Wolf's drool.

Wolf kept pulling at her. "You want me to run? Now?"

Wolf barked. He ran ahead of her and then stopped looking back as if to say come on. Alice got to her feet, feeling her way. After a few deep breaths, the dizziness eased a little. She couldn't run but she'd walk right out of here. She'd go to Miss Lawlor. The Dentons were closer, but she didn't know if Pa Denton was there. He would drive her back to the Ackermans. If Ma was alone, she would help her, but it was too much of a risk. Miss Lawlor would protect her. She had to get to town.

Wolf came running back to her, running around her trying to get her to move faster. But the ground kept spinning up to meet her if she moved too fast.

"Wolf slow down boy, we have to walk. He isn't due back until the weekend. We will have time. Walk slowly, that's better."

Wolf barked, his head butting her hand as she petted him. She wished she had gone back to get a drink and check on Eliza. It was too late now. She felt weak, and she had to get to town before darkness fell.

CHAPTER 26

Wolf stayed by her side, not running ahead like he would have done in the past. Occasionally he head-butted her gently as if to push her forward. She wanted to sit down and rest, to sleep but he wouldn't let her. Every time she tried, he barked and pulled at her clothes. She had no option but to keep going, one foot in front of the other.

The sun sank lower in the sky as she walked. She could see the roof of the schoolhouse in the distance, but it seemed to move away from her rather than coming closer. Wolf growled as a wagon came down the road behind them. Alice didn't know what to do, the road ahead was clear, there was nowhere for her to hide. What if the person driving the wagon insisted she go back to the Ackermans?

To her relief it was Jack. He jumped down, patting Wolf on the head as he did so. The dog didn't bark but licked his hand.

"Alice, what are ... What happened to you?" Jack took a step closer. He put his hand up to her cheek. Did He do this? I'll kill him."

"Jack, can you take me to Miss Lawlor? Please, I need to see her."

Jack helped her into the wagon. Wolf didn't join her but stayed on the road beside them. Once they got to the edge of town, Wolf lay down near the schoolhouse.

"Why isn't he coming?" Alice asked Jack.

"Probably knows most town folk fear a big dog like him. Especially as Ackerman spread the word, he is a killer. I got to find Miss Lawlor. You are awful white, Alice."

Alice tried to smile, but it hurt too much. She prayed hard Miss Lawlor was in the little house at the back of the schoolroom.

"Jack, I thought I heard a wagon. Alice, oh my goodness what happened to you. Jack?"

"Found her like this on the road. She said she was coming to you."

"Help her down, gently. Alice you're bleeding. Jack go for Doc Bester, tell him I'll pay. Go on now. I will look after Alice."

Alice let Miss Lawlor lead her to her house, grateful for the teacher's arm as the world had spun again. Her stomach heaved as she pushed Miss Lawlor out of the way.

"Poor child, what happened to you?"

"Visit from Miss Castle. Father's name is Weber, Gustav Weber. Think the older woman told Eliza who complained. Came to warn you. It was you wasn't it?"

Miss Lawlor flushed but shook her head. "No Alice, I didn't betray your trust, I promise."

"Doesn't matter now. I think she's dead. She wasn't moving. Wolf attacked her." The black spots danced in front of her eyes, but she fought against them.

"Don't worry about that for now. Come in and lie still. Jack will be back with the doctor in any minute. I'm just going to get a cloth and some water to wash that muck away. Then he can see what he's doing. Scalp wounds bleed a lot so don't be frightened."

On and on she talked, Alice wasn't sure what Miss Lawlor was saying as her voice went low and high, but she didn't care. Nobody could hurt her if Miss Lawlor was with her. She closed her eyes, wondering if her real father was looking for her right this minute.

CHAPTER 27

Maria moved her feet trying to ignore her hunger pains. Mama was doing her best producing a hot meal every evening. More often than not it was beans and pasta. Closing her eyes, Maria let herself imagine being back in Sicily enjoying a rare meat feast. As she daydreamed, she thought she heard a few people praying. Opening her eyes, she spotted a few Italian girls gathered around someone, their hands held together as they prayed. A rosary? She couldn't believe her eyes. It was a priest, a real one. Father António. What was he doing at the picket line?

She moved closer to hear him better, listening

with open mouth as he condemned the strike as an act against God.

"I think he's confusing God with some factory owners." One of the Jewish girls joked. But Maria wasn't laughing. This was serious. She looked at the other Italians faces. Some of them were listening intently to the priest. They were brought up to believe a man of the cloth. But why was the priest really here? Surely, he couldn't believe that God would want them to live like this. Could he?

She kept her distance not wanting Father Antonio to have any reason to notice her. All she needed was him visiting Mama. He'd persuade her, Maria should join Rosa in the Triangle Waist Factory. Shuddering at the thought of being on the ninth floor of any building, Maria took refuge behind some taller Jewish girls. She was thrilled to see Frieda walking along the street. Whispering to her friends, she would be back soon, she walked to meet Frieda.

"Thank goodness you are here. I have to disappear until Father António leaves."

"Have you had anything to eat? Lily gave me a nickel and I have some dimes too. We could get some soup and maybe bread?"

"Lead on. I could eat a horse today. Why are

you here? I thought you were studying for your exams."

"I was, but I got a note to say Sarah wanted to see us. We are to meet her outside Macy's."

"She's found Alice's father?" Maria threw her arms around Frieda. "That's amazing news."

"Maria, we don't know yet. She could want to speak about the strike."

Maria's hopes fell away. Frieda was right. She wanted to hear good news for once and if that had nothing to do with the strike, it would be even better. She was sick of feeling hungry and cold. She was fed up with the arguments with her mother and Rosa. The strike was worth it but it would be nice to escape just for a little while.

They walked in silence to Macy's where they spotted an older man with Sarah. He was flushed, talking with his hands in an animated fashion. Sarah caught sight of them, the look of relief on her face was almost comical.

"Mr. Weber, these are the ladies I was telling you about. Frieda and Maria, meet Mr. Gustav Weber."

"You have my girl, my Alice?" Mr. Gustav burst out before saying something in German.

Frieda answered in German.

Maria didn't have a clue what she said. She glanced at the man who looked more anguished if possible.

"Come inside and sit down. It's too cold to chat out here." Frieda suggested. Maria glanced at Sarah, neither of them could afford to have a drink in Macy's. Before they could protest, Frieda ushered them inside. "Lily's treat. Come on."

Maria followed eager to hear what Mr. Weber had to say. Was Alice his daughter and if so how could he have put her into an orphanage.

They took seats at a table with Frieda ordering soup and bread for everyone. Maria's stomach growled making them all laugh.

"Mine does that too, Miss Please don't look so embarrassed." Mr. Weber said as she turned scarlet. Then he spoke again to Frieda, but she asked him to speak in English for Maria's benefit.

"Does your daughter have any identifying marks?" Frieda asked.

"Ya, since the fire. Her hair, it burned and left a scar here." The man gestured to the back of his head. "My wife, Agatha…" The man squeezed his eyes shut for a second before he continued, "she pushed Alice into the water. Then she jumped after her. She held Alice, trying to save her from the flames. But still my little girl got injured. And my wife….she didn't survive."

"Were you on the boat?"

"No, I was working. I should have taken the day off. My Agatha, she wanted me to but I said no. Boss would be angry. If I had been there, maybe…"

"Mr. Weber, my father was with us and still my brother died. My father couldn't save us. You should stop blaming yourself."

"But it is not just that. I left Alice in the hospital, she was very badly hurt. I had to work. I asked for help. They said they would keep Alice until she got better and then she could come home. I took a job out of New York, the money was better and I wanted to give Alice a good home. Also being around Little Germany was too painful with the memories. When I got back, Alice wasn't in the hospital. Nobody knew where she was. I searched high and low but nothing. Nobody had seen my girl. The nuns at the hospital, they say it was better for everyone. But it wasn't, not for me and not for Alice. But you think you have found her?"

Maria choked on her tears, unable to swallow her soup. The poor man, to lose his wife and then his child.

Frieda took his hands in hers. "Mr. Weber, we

think we may have found Alice. A girl matching her description is living with a family in a place called Deadman's Creek. Her teacher wrote to my friend about her. She is helping Alice find her father. Alice remembered his name was Gustav."

"Ya, me. Gustav. I must go to her." He stood up and then sat back down again. "What am I thinking? I can't go now. I need to have a home for her and money for food, clothes and everything a girl needs."

Sarah intervened. "Gustav joined the strike. Most of the men in his factory did."

"Mr. Weber, Alice can stay with us at the Sanctuary. Why don't you come and meet Lily and Kathleen, who are both involved with the orphan trains."

"These women, they sent my Alice away?"

"No, they've never met Alice. Finish your soup and I will fill you in on the whole story as we walk back to the Sanctuary. Maria, Sarah do you want to come too?"

Sarah answered, "I'd love to but I have to get back to the picket. Maria you coming?"

"I can't be too long away from the picket line. I don't want the other Italian girls to think I am afraid of that priest."

"Priest?" Frieda asked between mouthfuls of soup.

"He spoke at the picket line this morning. You should have heard him. He was talking about all sorts of sins. The priest says he will go visit our parents. You know what they will say. No Italian child is allowed to disrespect their parents. I can just hear Mama now. What will the neighbors say? As if that was important."

"Frieda, stop fretting. I heard Arturio Caroti and Salvatore Ninfo are getting involved." Sarah pushed aside her bowl, looking like she had washed it clean.

Maria"s eyes widened. "They are? Papa has heard of those men. Who hasn't? They are famous."

"Yes, and they are on our side. I've heard they are calling to families and speaking to the parents."

Gustav grunted. "Speaking is cheap. It won't put bread on the table or pasta in the pot. A neighbor boiled hot water on the fire. She said she had to pretend to the neighbors she was cooking for her family. She cried so much. I wouldn't dismiss the efforts of the church to get the Italians back on shift."

"Do you agree, Maria? How much trouble do you think it will cause?" Sarah asked.

Maria hated giving Sarah bad news, but she had to be honest.

"I think quite a few of the girls will go back to work. I don't know what it is like for you with your holy men but in Italy a priest's word is law. There aren't many families who will go against the church." Maria wasn't at all sure she could stay on the picket lines now.

A speculative gleam lit up Sarah's eyes. "Including your own?"

Maria bowed her head. "Yes Sarah. I think I should go home now. Just in case."

"Try to persuade your parents we have to stick with this. If we fail now, we will never get proper working conditions."

"I know Sarah but with Rosa working at the Triangle and bringing home tales of hot soup and apple tart for lunchtime and her earnings, it's hard."

"Maria, I know the Triangle. Those things, the music and everything will disappear as fast as the picket lines do when this is over. Believe me. Then your sister will have to face working with locked doors and stupid rules. I should know. I worked there."

Gustav nodded. "It is as Sarah says."

Maria stood up and together they all walked out of Macy's. Mr. Weber and Frieda heading in the Sanctuary's direction, with Maria and Sarah walking back toward the picket lines.

"Don't lose faith my Italian friend. We have fought too hard to give up now. Go home now. I expect to see you on the picket lines tomorrow."

Maria wished she shared her friend's faith. She was right to worry. By the time she got home it was too late. Father António had got there first. Mama was crying and Papa was pacing the floor.

"Maria, you must start working with Rosa. This strike has gone on long enough. We tried to support you, but we can't do it anymore. Father António says…"

"Mama, I can't back out now. We are close to winning. The priest doesn't understand. How can he? Did he look underfed to you? Did he look like he was eating pasta and beans day in and day out?"

Papa's shout made her jump.

"Maria Josephina Agnesca Mezza, don't you talk about the priest like that. Show some respect for the church and your mother."

Maria could have screamed, but she bowed her head. "Sorry Papa, Mama. I didn't mean to be disrespectful." She counted to ten in silence before adding, "Can't you see? If we go back to work now and break the strike, they have won. Twenty thousand people support the strike. Twenty thousand."

Her Papa sank into his chair, his breathing more labored than ever. Mama wiped her eyes with her handkerchief over and over, twisting it in her fingers. Maria's heart felt like it was being torn from her chest. She glanced up to see Louisa and Sophie staring at her from the bedroom, Louisa had her thumb in her mouth and her hand wrapped in Sophie's. Both looked terrified. She couldn't do this to her family. She sighed and sat down.

"I will work with Rosa if that's what you want."

Mama smiled perilously through the tears grabbing her hands and kissing them. "You are a good girl Maria. Isn't she Papa?"

Maria glanced at her father, terrified to see his eyes glistening. Papa never cried, well apart from the day they left his mother back in Sicily. It was coming up to the anniversary of her death, one year since the earthquake and Tsunami that had destroyed their village and killed most of their family they'd left behind in Messina.

"Papa, please don't get upset. I will go now to

wait for Rosa and speak to the foreman to start tomorrow."

Maria pushed the chair back, but her father grabbed her hand, surprising her with his strength. He spoke rapidly in Sicilian.

"No. You wait until after Christmas. We will give you until January 2nd. By then your strike may be over, yes?"

She answered him back in her native language trying to make promises she couldn't keep. "Yes, Papa, I don't think it will last much longer. People are running out of money, a girl I met today told me her mother has been boiling water to pretend to her neighbors she is feeding her family. There will be others like that. But please let me try for a little while longer."

Papa rubbed her hand in his, but he spoke to his wife. Maria was astonished to hear him talk about Caroti and Ninfo. He'd heard the talk about them providing strike relief.

"No Papa, I won't take charity from no-one." Mama's protest was all the stronger as she spoke in English. She did this when she was trying to be American.

"I am head of this household and I say we will." Papa pushed his chair back. "I will go see the men upstairs, to listen to some intelligent conversation."

The door slammed shut behind him leaving silence. Maria was almost afraid to look at her mother. The sound of pans banging told her all she needed to know. She crept into the bedroom and closed the door before pulling both her sisters into an embrace. "Here, Frieda sent you a little present." She gave the girls some broken candy. "It will be fine, don't worry. Things will blow over and mama and papa will be back to normal in a few hours."

At dinner that evening, nobody commented on the pasta and beans. Papa stayed silent but mama sniffed regularly. Maria risked a glance at her mother, seeing her tears glistening in her eyes, the red trail on her face. Guilt flooded through her. Was she doing the right thing? Rosa was late home. Their parents assumed she was working but her sister confided she had gone walking with Paulo. Maria hoped for Rosa's sake their parents didn't get to hear of her antics. She didn't think they could weather much more. She wondered if Frieda and Gustav were getting on any better.

CHAPTER 28

"Lily and Kathleen, good you are here. I'd like to introduce you to someone. This is Gustav Weber, we think he might be Alice's father."

Lily and Kathleen exchanged looks sending a chill through Frieda. "What is it? What's wrong?"

"Let's ring for some tea. It will help." Kathleen suggested, before shaking Mr. Weber's hand.

"Please, no tea. Just tell me if my daughter, Alice, is safe."

Frieda stared at Kathleen's face, it was paler than Lily's and that was saying something. "What happened?"

Lily held out a letter. "Please sit down and I will read it to you. It came last week but I didn't see it until this afternoon. It was hidden behind some papers."

Gustav sat awkwardly on the edge of a seat but Frieda remained standing.

Lily read the letter.

Dear Kathleen,

Thank you so much for answering my letter. It would appear something you did in New York prompted the Orphan Society to take action.

They sent two of their inspectors to visit Alice at home. I don't like to speak badly about people but, to be frank, the senior inspector is not someone I would judge as being suitable to work with children. She had rather a mean disposition. She told me in no uncertain terms I should mind my business or lose my position as the children's teacher. She said Alice was lucky to have such a wonderful home with people born to be parents. Mrs. Ackerman may have been born with a special purpose, but that of mother to any child particularly a vulnerable young girl wasn't it.

But that doesn't matter. Alice has run away with a boy from the class, Jack Denton. He is a very mature, sensible young man who will do his best to look after Alice. Nobody knows where they've gone, not even Jack's twin brother.

Mrs. Ackerman is in the hospital. Her husband's dog attacked her on the same day of the visit.

The town council didn't appreciate my intervention and have left me with no option but to leave Deadman's Creek. I will join my fiancé next week. This is my forwarding address.

Miss April Lawlor
c/o Fort Sheridan
Illinois.

If by any miracle, you come across Alice, please give her a hug from me. She is a very special young lady.

Yours sincerely
April Lawlor

Mr. Weber said something inaudible in German.

"Kathleen, I don't believe it. How could she just leave when Alice is missing? The poor child. She must be on her way to New York." Frieda paced back and forth.

Kathleen sat holding the letter. She read it again and again. "Frieda, Lily, I think this letter is a message. Miss Lawlor wrote it, that's her handwriting for sure. But the tone is so different from the first letter she sent. I think she was trying to tell us something."

Lily retorted. "She did. The child ran away, but she doesn't care as she is going back to her fiancé to get married."

"Lily, don't you think that is out of character? I mean we don't know her but that doesn't sound like the first lady who wrote to us. Does it?"

Lily took the letter, put her glasses on read it.

"You mean she has written it like this in case it got into the wrong hands?"

Kathleen leaned forward in her chair. "Yes, that's exactly what I mean. What if Miss Lawlor helped Alice escape? Maybe Alice is making her way to New York to us?"

Lily glanced at the letter again before looking up at Kathleen. "Why not send us a letter to tell us?"

"I don't know Lily but maybe Miss Lawlor is scared. You read what she said about the Ackermans being respected by the local townspeople. Could she be afraid her letter might not reach us? Someone could intercept it."

"Kathleen Green, you are reading too many detective stories. Nobody would interfere with the mail, that's a serious crime."

Frieda eagerly grasped the line of hope Kathleen offered. "Only if you get caught. If you were a sheriff trying to find out the whereabouts of a runaway child, you could exert your authority."

Kathleen glanced at Gustav. "Mr. Weber, I'm sorry we don't have better news for you. Do you know of anywhere Alice would go if she came back to New York?"

Helpless, he stared back at them and shook his head.

"I do." Frieda cried. "I went back to my home in Little Germany. I had to check for myself my father and my brother were no longer there. Alice could do the same."

Mr. Weber looked more desolate if possible.

"Our home doesn't exist. Lots of people moved away and the town planners or whatever they call them, said they needed to build a factory. They've only got as far as pulling down the old building."

"Don't worry Mr. Weber. You aren't alone in this. We will all help and we will get Maria, Sarah and her friends to help too. Lily and Kathleen know some very important people including a police inspector. If anyone can find Alice, we can."

"Well said Frieda. Mr. Weber where are you living now?"

Mr. Weber colored before standing. "Here and there, I don't have a fixed address."

Frieda rushed to save the man from embarrassment. "Mr. Weber joined the strike. Sarah said he led the men from his factory to join us."

"I have seen what happens when there are no rules or nobody obeys the rules. I just did my duty."

Lily shook his hand. "I can't offer you a room here as it is a woman's only sanctuary, Mr. Weber but you are welcome to come home to my house.

My husband, Charlie, will help me find you lodgings."

"Thank you, but I won't impose."

Kathleen stepped forward. "It's almost Christmas. Go with Lily, Mr. Weber. The streets are no place to spend Christmas and we need to know where you are. Just in case we get word about Alice."

He looked uncertain as if torn over the decision. Frieda knew pride would stop him from taking charity. She glanced at Lily.

"Please, Mr. Weber. I feel somewhat responsible for Alice going missing. I told a dear friend, a priest about her and he contacted the orphan society. Maybe if they hadn't visited, Alice would still be with Miss Lawlor."

Frieda could have cheered. Trust Lily to blame herself, thereby hoping Mr. Weber would want to make her feel better. But still the man was wavering.

It was time for some tough love. Frieda summoned her doctor's voice, the one that gave clear commands. "Mr. Weber, you won't get Alice back if you don't have a home for her. When she arrives in New York, she will need you."

Kathleen gasped, sending Frieda a look of reproach. Kathleen opened her mouth to say something but Frieda shook her head. Frieda watched Mr. Weber, his glassy eyes testament to his feelings.

Mr. Weber rubbed his eyes with his sleeve leaving a line of grime. "Thank you, thank you all. Miss Lily, it would honor me to visit your home."

Frieda exhaled a breath she hadn't realized she was holding. Now the next job was to find Alice and bring her home.

CHAPTER 29

Alice groaned struggling against the nauseous feeling, the pain in her head caused. The house smelled different; it was like... Christmas. Ginger mixed with boiled cabbage and roast meat.

"Alice, are you awake?"

Alice opened her eyes to the soft voice. This wasn't the house she'd lived in. It was much smaller. She was lying in a small bed near an open fire. She saw a closed door off to the left and a curtained off area to the right. The stove was behind the figure above her. She tried to concentrate, the blurry image gradually taking focus. Ma Denton loomed over her, concern written all over her face. "Please Alice, wake up. You've slept through Christmas."

Alice gave up trying to move her head, the pain was too bad. She raised her hand to Ma's face. "Why am I here?"

"Thank God. You gave us such a fright. Doc warned about infection. You had too many open wounds. Miss Lawlor, she bought the best medicines money could buy. She bought us food too. Can you smell the beef? Can you get out of bed?"

Alice tried to lift her head. She fought past the pain and the dizziness wanting to bring a smile to Ma's face.

"Jack, Jacob, Pa. Come quick, Alice's awake."

The boys and their father came running at Ma's shout.

"Praise the lord." Pa Denton muttered.

"About time, Alice. We thought you were a goner. Now can I tell the other kids at school, Ma?"

"No, you keep your mouth shut Jacob or I'll shut if for you."

Alice stared at Jack, she'd never heard him threaten anyone before never mind his twin. She glanced at Ma and saw the look of terror on her face before Ma caught her looking and gave her a tight smile.

"What's wrong? Why are you scared?" She closed her eyes as images flew into her head. She tried to make sense of them. Eliza was on the ground at the house. Maria was in a wagon, Miss Lawlor was crying. Wolf helping her. Wolf? Where was he?

"Wolf?"

"He's outside chewing on a bone. Darn dog is useless. He won't leave the front door. Least he's stopped whimpering now." Tobacco juice dribbled out the side of Pa's mouth as he spoke. "Reckon this deserves a drink."

"Pa, you can't go to town. They'll be asking questions."

"It's Saturday night woman. All the men will have a drink. There'll be more questions if I don't go. Reckon that fancy teacher lady will be around soon. Don't like the way she looks at me. She's rather uppity for a woman."

Alice saw Ma purse her lips, but the woman didn't respond. Alice curled her hands around Ma's hand.

"Pa, don't go saying nothing about Alice." Jack stepped forward and stood head to head with his Pa. Alice gasped. Pa Denton had a temper. She didn't want Jack to get hurt. Pa's temper flared, he flexed his hands into fists and took a step nearer his son.

Jack didn't move. Pa's eyes widened, his face flushed.

"Mr. Denton, thank you for saving me." Alice whispered. Her diversion worked as the man looked at her. Her kindness seemed to confuse him.

"T'was nothing," he muttered before he made a move toward the door.

"Here, buy yourself a whiskey to celebrate." Ma took a coin from her apron and pressed it into his hand. To Alice's surprise, he kissed his wife, telling her she was the best. He slapped her behind making her blush like a young girl. Alice glanced at Jack to see his reaction but he was staring into the fire.

"Jack?"

Jack turned as she called his name. He came closer to the bed.

"What happened to Eliza? Is she dead?" Alice whispered.

"No, she's in the hospital. Dr. said she will get better but it will take a while. She broke her leg and her arm."

"And him?"

Jack scowled. "Ned Ackerman's been making

things difficult for Miss Lawlor. He reckons she helped you to run away. Miss Lawlor wrote a letter to those people in New York saying you did and she doesn't know where you are. Ackerman doesn't believe her even though he saw the letter."

"How?" Alice knew letters were private.

"Sheriff gave it to him."

"The sheriff?"

"Yeah, his job is to find you and get you back to the Ackermans."

Alice tried to sit up, fighting her weakness, but it was pointless.

"You stay where you are. Another few days and you'll be stronger. Then we leave."

"We do?"

"Yes, Miss Lawlor has it all figured out. She's leaving in three days to get married. She's coming here later to tell us the plan."

Alice wanted to know the plan now but her eyes were closing. Every inch of her hurt, her legs almost more than her head.

"Alice, I'm so glad you woke up. You scared the heck out of me. Sleep now. You need to get better."

Alice opened her eyes to see Jack gazing at her,

a look of tenderness of his face. She smiled, and that was the last she remembered.

* * *

Whispering woke her up sometime later. She'd been having a nice dream about her parents. She saw her father's face as he hoisted her onto his shoulders. They were walking with a lady. She couldn't see the lady's face but heard her laughing.

There were lots of other families strolling with them. The sun was shining and everyone was excited and then she heard the voices.

"Jack, I've paid your Pa to take you to the station at Weir Falls. They are watching the one in Deadwood Creek. These are your tickets to Chicago. I couldn't buy you ones to New York as it would be too easy to track you down."

Alice knew that voice. Miss Lawlor was here. She pushed through the cloud of pain to open her eyes. "Miss Lawlor." Her shout came out as a whisper but it was enough to get their attention.

"Alice, my brave girl. Thank God for Christmas miracles."

Alice stared at the teacher. She looked different, older and strained. Her smile didn't hide the worry in her eyes.

"Thank you. Jack said you saved me."

"I did nothing, Alice. Mrs. Denton gave you a home and has nursed you back to health with some help from the Doc."

"Are you leaving?"

A tear slid down Miss Lawlor's cheek before she brushed it out of the way. "I have to, Alice. Every day I spend here, I put you at risk. I wish I could take you to New York."

"You can."

"No, darling Alice, I can't. Mr. Ackerman will follow me. He's convinced I am hiding you somewhere. He doesn't know of my friendship with Mrs. Denton."

Jacob burst out laughing. "You should have seen Ma in town Alice. She gave Miss Lawlor a smack across the face. Left her all red and Miss Lawlor was crying and everything."

Horrified Alice glanced at Ma and then at Miss Lawlor who rubbed her face.

"Don't ever get on the wrong side of Mrs. Denton, Alice. She has a mean left hook."

Ma Denton colored up. "I'm so sorry, April.

I didn't mean to hit you hard, but you said it had to look realistic."

"I know Mary. You did a wonderful job, and it was my idea not yours. You see Alice, if people saw us fighting in the street, they wouldn't dream Mrs. Denton was hiding you."

Alice couldn't take it all in. It seemed very complicated.

"Alice, this is my new address. I've given Mrs. Denton money for you and Jack. It should be enough for the train tickets. When you get to New York, this is the address you go to."

"Is Miss Baker there?"

Miss Lawlor shook her head. "I couldn't trace Miss Baker, Alice. These are the friends I wrote to, who are looking for your father. I'm hopeful they'll have good news for you. I wish I could travel with you."

"I do too." Alice muttered.

Jack sat on the bed beside her, taking her hand. "There's something else, Alice. We can't bring Wolf."

Alice pulled away from him. "No, I'm not losing Wolf. If he doesn't go, I'm not either."

Miss Lawlor and Ma Denton went outside the house to talk but Alice didn't care what they said.

Wolf was her family. He'd protected her, and she wasn't going anywhere without him. She gritted her teeth and tried to get out of bed.

"What are you doing?"

"Getting out of bed, Jack. You said I had to get my strength back. Wolf will help me. Wolf?" She called. The dog was by her side in seconds, licking her feet. He didn't jump up on her but nuzzled her hand with his head. She laughed, as he tickled her.

"See, he's good for me. I need him, Jack. I can't leave him behind."

Jack looked away but not before she saw his eyes watering. Before she got to act, the adults came back in.

"Guess we couldn't keep you too apart if we tried. Wolf will follow your trail and may even give the game away. He must travel in the wagon too but you must keep him quiet and out of sight. Alice, Jack, it's important."

"We will, Miss Lawlor. Wolf will do as he's told. Won't you boy?"

Wolf barked in response. Then he lay at Alice's feet, his eyes looking at her in adoration.

"He'll be a good guard dog. I hate to think of them alone in Chicago. It's a big city."

"My Jack won't let anything happen to Alice." Ma Denton put her hand on his shoulder.

Jack sat straighter. "I'll be back soon as I give her to those people in New York. You won't even know I've gone."

"I will but I know you got to do this. Now, how about some lunch? Alice would you like some soup?"

Alice shook her head. "I'd like some gingerbread cookies."

CHAPTER 30

CHRISTMAS DAY 1909

Christmas Day passed without even a tree to grace the apartment let alone Mama's favorite gingerbread cookies. Benito was staying with his wife's mother this year but sent his parents some tobacco for Papa and some gloves for Mama. The presents made Mama cry more. "I can't feed the children gloves. Why waste his money on these when we can't put food on the table?"

Maria didn't speak. She knew whatever she said would only inflame the situation. Rosa pinched her hard. "See what you have done. All my earnings go to the rent and now we have to sit in the cold without food because of your principles. You need to get a job Maria and fast. Papa is worse and now Mama too. If anything happens to them, I will never forgive you. Paulo thinks you need a good slap to bring you to your senses."

"You tell your Paulo to keep his hands to himself. Nobody not a jumped-up Mafiosi will tell me what to do. Papa says I have until January 2nd."

Maria stormed out of the apartment and walked and walked to get rid of her frustration. If Paulo Greco put a hand on her, she'd tell the cops all about him and his black-market dealings. She was almost certain he earned some money from breaking up the picket lines. She'd heard rumors he liked to hit the Jewish girls, but she'd never met a victim. Not one that identified herself. People knew her sister was walking out with Greco. That was enough to keep most silent. The arm of the Mafia spread wide across the Sicilian and Italian community.

Snow fell. Maria pulled her shawl closer over her hand, wishing she had remembered her gloves. A wagon passed and sprayed her with the dirty water from the road. Miserable, she shivered as she made her way home hoping her parents would have found their Christmas spirit.

* * *

ORPHAN TRAIN STRIKE

THREE DAYS LATER, she found herself on a street corner selling copies of "The Call", the official newspaper. It usually cost two cents, but this special edition was a nickel, but some people pressed more money into her hand. The support was nice, but she wished it was from her family rather than strangers. Nobody at home was talking to her now. Papa wouldn't speak to anyone and everyone blamed her.

"Maria, how are you? I missed you over Christmas. Here, these are for you."

Maria spun around at the sound of Frieda's voice. She unwrapped the present to find an apple and a pair of warm gloves. "One lady knit several pairs and I thought of you. It's cold out here. I'll take a newspaper too. Lily gave me a dollar for you."

Maria put on the gloves before she handed over the copy of the newspaper.

"So, what's happening?" Frieda asked.

"Have you heard the Associated Waist and Dress manufacturers offered a deal? They will impose the 52-hour week. They won't charge for needles or supplies either."

"Maria, that's wonderful, you won. You should smile yet you look so unhappy. What's wrong?"

"The Union rejected it. They say they won't take a deal unless the factory owners agree to a closed shop. Frieda, what if they don't? I can't see the girls lasting much longer. Papa told me I have to go to work with Rosa at the Triangle if things aren't settled by January 2nd. That's next week."

Maria hated admitting defeat, but she couldn't see any other way. She waited for Frieda to reassure her, but her friend hesitated.

"What's wrong? You have that look on your face, Frieda. Tell me."

"I don't know anything, not for certain but I heard Lily and Kathleen talking. They said Anne Morgan and her friends might not be agreeable to the strike continuing if you got most of your demands. It's a big victory getting them to agree to the 52-hour week. And to set hours. Did you hear some factories have installed cot beds for their scab workers, so they don't have to pass the picket lines. They're determined not to let you win, Maria." Frieda stared at the ground not attempting to meet Maria's eyes.

"You agree with them? The rich women!" Maria retorted. She immediately regretted doing so as the hurt flared in Frieda's eyes. "Frieda, ignore me. I shouldn't be taking my frustration out on you. I'm sorry for speaking to you like that."

Frieda waved away her apology. "Maria, I know how hard you've worked but can't you see you've won? Not on every point, but it's a start. I know your family has had it tough but at least Rosa is working. Your mother too, making those artificial flowers you mentioned. Some families have no money coming in. They have lost everything. It might be time to say enough."

Maria kicked the sidewalk just like a five-year-old child would. She couldn't help it and it was better than screaming. Frieda was right, and they both knew it. Her friend had only voiced Maria's own feelings. She thought the union had been short-sighted to turn down the offer too. Not that she would admit that.

"Now can you come and find a hot drink with me? I need cheering up. I can't stop worrying about Alice."

"What can you do, Frieda?"

"Nothing for the moment. We can't do anything anyway not until Alice turns up." Frieda took a sip of her coffee. "How are things at home? How is your father?"

"Struggling but he won't see a doctor or go back to the hospital."

"I will try to call to see him. But maybe it's best he avoids the hospital. We have another outbreak of Typhoid. I thought by locking up Typhoid Mary they would reduce the number of cases but, oh listen to me go on. I was supposed to cheer you up not make you even more unhappy."

Maria hugged her friend impulsively. "Your friendship always cheers me up. Go on, back to work and be careful. We don't want you catching anything."

"Don't worry Maria. Things will work out, they always do."

Maria watched Frieda until she disappeared from view. If only she had her friend's optimism.

* * *

Maria climbed the steps to the tenement, every step making her toes tingle as they defrosted. She'd spent another five hours on the picket lines. She was used to being tired but, in the past, she'd believed in what they were fighting for. After speaking to

Frieda, she wondered if the unions were wrong. They had achieved some victories.

"About time you showed your face." Rosa spat.

"Leave me be, please." Maria shut the door behind her only then realizing the girls were alone. "Where's Mama? Papa?"

"At the hospital. Papa took a turn, he couldn't breathe. The doctor came and ordered an ambulance. Mama followed. Left Louisa and Sophia here, *alone,* until I came home. Mama thought you would be back sooner. You're the one without a job."

Maria ignored Rosa's sniping. Doctors only called ambulances in emergencies. "Which hospital?" she turned toward the door as she spoke. Rosa's hand wrenched her back.

"Oh, no you don't. You stay here and listen to me. Get a job. Papa can't get better on pasta and beans. He needs sardines and fresh bread, eggs and potatoes. Most of all he has to stop worrying about paying our bills. You can change this, Maria, if you stopped being selfish and went back to sewing where you belong."

"Papa agreed with the strike."

"Papa can't agree with anything anymore. He

can't even breathe." Rosa brushed the tears away, but they kept flowing.

It was Rosa's tears that decided the issue. Maria was used to her sister's rants, pinches and threats. But not her tears. Rosa didn't cry.

"Maria, please. You could get a good job with me at the Triangle. I spoke to Anna Gullo–she's my forelady. She won't tell you were in the strikes. She knows I'm a good worker, and I told her you were even better."

Maria glanced at her sister.

"It's true. We both know you learn faster than I do. So, now's your chance to earn more money. They will pay you more than old Reinhardt. Come back now before everyone else and you will get the pick of the machines. Near the window. What do you say? The two of us working together again will please Mama. We can buy eggs. Louisa and Sophia will like that won't you girls?"

Their younger siblings stayed mute. They stared at Maria with their big brown eyes. When had they got so thin? Their little faces were pinched with the cold, no wonder as the apartment was freezing. Maria shuddered, feeling a hundred years older. Rosa was right. She couldn't continue striking. Her family needed her.

She sat without taking her coat off. "I will go back to work."

Rosa threw her arms around her, nearly knocking Maria backward off her chair. "I knew you would see sense." Before her sister got carried away, Maria said.

"Rosa, I can't work at the Triangle. I hate being so far off the ground." Working on the 8th, 9th or 10th floor of a building terrified her. She didn't even like heights.

"Don't be silly. The building is the best factory. It's made of stone so is safe. Anyway, Reinhardt won't employ you on your old wages. He'll take advantage. He knows what you did, you didn't just stay on the picket lines, you got involved at all levels in the strike. He'll make you pay for that. Anna Gullo will turn a blind eye. Work with me. We need the money, all of us are hungry and cold, Papa most of all."

It was a low ball, and they both knew it. Maria loved her parents, but she was a daddy's girl. Papa understood her love of reading and learning, her dreams of being more than a shirtwaist worker. Papa who'd sacrificed so much in taking them to America. He'd saved their lives as they most likely would have died if they'd stayed in Sicily, in the earthquake that killed their grandmother, aunts, uncles, cousins and friends last year.

"I will go with you tomorrow, Rosa."

"I knew you'd see sense. Louisa, start a small fire. I'll run up to Mama Midolo to borrow some food. We know we can pay her back now Maria's back earning."

Rosa almost fell in her race out the apartment door. Louisa hugged Maria. "Thank you."

Her little sister's simple thanks was her undoing. She mumbled an excuse and leaving her sisters to follow Rosa's instructions, Maria walked into their bedroom and closed the door behind her. The tears fell, and she did not stop them. How could she have put her family through so much? If Papa didn't recover, she would never forgive herself.

CHAPTER 31

Maria didn't sleep that night, but it wasn't Rosa's gentle snoring keeping her awake. Mama had come home late from the hospital with Benito. Her brother's face confirmed Maria's fears. Papa was so ill, Mama didn't seem to register the news she was returning to work. Benito did. He asked her to walk him downstairs as he had to get back to his pregnant wife and children. Benito spoke rapidly in Sicilian.

"Maria, I know you didn't want to do this, but it's best for the family. Papa has been too lenient."

Maria bristled but didn't argue. Let Benito think she was listening. He didn't live with them, didn't contribute to the family so it was none of his business.

"Papa will not live for long. The doctors say a day or two. Look after Mama. Rosa will marry Greco as soon as she can."

"Stop it Benito. You talk like he is dead already. Doctor Green will make Papa better. I know he will."

She didn't wait for his response but ran inside back to Mama and her sisters. She prayed all night for a miracle. She'd do anything for Papa to live and if that meant working on the 9th floor of the Asch building, that's what she would do. Despite her best intentions, every time she closed her eyes, nightmares came. She was being driven out of the factory by the police who wanted to put in the workhouse with Mama and the little ones.

"Come on sleepy head, let's go. We need to be early. Can't risk anyone recognizing you and making a fuss. If the bosses find out you are a striker, even Anna can't save you."

Maria didn't reply. She washed her face in the ice-cold water to wake up. Mama was asleep at the kitchen table, a mound of unfinished flowers in front of her. She kissed her tear-stained face. "Papa will come home, Mama."

Mama looked at her, the dull acceptance in her

eyes frightening Maria. Rosa didn't have to call her twice.

The walk to the Asch building took over an hour. It was chilly but at least it wasn't raining. "See Washington Park is right over there. When the weather gets warmer, we can sit in the park at lunchtime. Stop frowning Maria. It's a good job and we get our lunches. Anna is not like Reinhardt. She expects you to work hard, but she is not breathing over you like some pig." Rosa tried to laugh but it sounded false. Maria didn't even break a smile.

As she walked into the building, her breathing came in short bursts. She had to breathe slowly so as not to panic.

"Joseph, this is my sister Maria. She starts today. Maria, Joseph will bring us up and down."

Maria returned Joseph's Italian greeting and then hugged the side of the elevator as it started its upward journey. She closed her eyes at every noise praying silently until it stopped at the 9th floor.

"Have a good day, ladies, nice meeting you Maria."

Thrilled to be back on solid ground, Maria followed Rosa into the room and stopped to stare around her in disbelief. Just how many machines were there? It looked like hundreds. She grabbed Rosa's coat.

"You didn't say there were so many working here."

Rosa looked around as if seeing the place for the first time.

"Almost two hundred and fifty machinists, at least there is when they aren't striking. Do you want to sit by the windows?" Rosa pointed out the row closest to the window, but Maria shook her head. She didn't want to know how high they were off the ground.

"I sit here, in the middle row. Clara, she's German, sits over there. They don't like us sitting near friends so why don't you take this one?" Rosa pointed to a machine near the door. Maria glanced around her, sixteen rows with fifteen machines on each row. "That is where you put your finished work." Rosa indicated the trough between Maria and the machinist sitting opposite her. "The wicker basket at your feet has your unfinished work. Anna likes everything neat and tidy." Rosa shrugged her shoulders. "As you can see, there isn't much room to move around, but it's not like we go dancing here, anyway." Rosa laughed at her own joke as she went to find Anna Gullo.

Maria stared around her, fighting the urge to flee out the door. She sat on the wooden chair in front of the wooden table and tried to get comfortable. She stood up again as soon as Rosa returned with what she assumed was the forelady.

"Morning Maria, I hope you are as good as Rosa says as I am taking a big risk putting you to work. I don't want no trouble, you hear?"

"Yes, ma'am."

The woman's face relaxed into a smile. "Good girl. Mr. Harris and Mr. Blanck aren't the dragons the press makes them out to be. Work hard and you will do just fine."

"Thank you, Mrs. Gullo."

The woman nodded before turning to Rosa. "I'm sure you can explain to your sister how everything works. I have to find Mary." The woman bustled off, her skirts rustling.

"Mary Leventhal distributes the bundles of cut work brought up from downstairs. She's nice enough."

Maria heard the unspoken words. Nice enough for someone not Italian... But she didn't comment. She needed Rosa's help.

***

THAT NIGHT, they left the factory and walked to the hospital. Papa was still breathing but one look at Doctor Green's face said everything.

"I am sorry, Papa. I should have gone back to work sooner. I'm so sorry." Maria cried, her head on his bed. Rosa had left to get Mama. Doctor Green said the crisis would come later that night.

"Don't...be...sorry. Proud of you." Papa gasped between each word.

"Don't speak Papa. Save your strength and fight back."

"Maria. Be strong. Mama...she fights with you. You strong..." Papa took a few breaths. "Hold the family together. Maria...promise me. Look after Rosa. Greco no good."

At his mention of Paulo, Papa grabbed her fingers tight, squeezing them hard. She hated Paulo even more at that minute for causing her papa pain.

Tears streaming down her face, Maria nodded and mumbled. "Yes Papa, I promise. I love you papa. I love you." She kept repeating it although he didn't speak again. She watched as his chest rose and fell, his breathing sounding horrible. With one last shuddering breath, he fell silent.

"Papa, nooooooo," she screamed, but he didn't wake up. She lay there sobbing until she heard her mama scream behind her.

"Benito, don't leave me. Benito wake up." Mama repeated the Sicilian words over and over. Maria moved to comfort her, but mama turned on her, eyes blazing.

"You. You did this with your stupid strike. Look at your papa. Not only did you kill him, but you stole my last moments with him. Get away, out of my sight."

Maria stumbled back as her mother pushed her. She'd have fallen over but for Frieda catching her.

"Come along Maria. I'll send someone to your mama."

Maria let Frieda lead her away, she couldn't speak. It was her fault, Papa was dead. Mama was right she had been stupid and selfish.

* * *

MARIA WAS SURPRISED to see the number of people who turned out for Papa's funeral. She spotted Frieda with Lily, Kathleen and both Dr's Green. She almost missed Mr. Weber. He gave her a gentle smile. The poor man still had no news of his daughter. Maria's eyes filled again. Now she had lost Papa, she could understand better how the loss of someone you loved hurt so badly. She closed to eyes to pray Mr. Weber would be reunited with his daughter one day soon.

CHAPTER 32

CHICAGO, FEBRUARY 1910

Wolf growled, his paw on Alice's back. She lay as still as possible, hugging the corner of the abandoned hut they'd been living in for the past week. The footsteps didn't belong to Jack, if they had Wolf wouldn't be standing up ready to pounce. She listened as the footsteps stopped but only for a few seconds, then the person moved on until she heard nothing.

"I'm glad you're with us, Wolf. I'd be so scared if you weren't here." Alice rubbed her head into his fur. She loved the dog more than most anything in the world.

Wolf barked. "Shush, we're supposed to be hiding." Alice waited for Jack's whistle. They'd agreed a system to keep them safe since the day

Jack got mugged and lost Miss Lawlor's savings. They'd have been in New York by now if that hadn't of happened. Jack was doing everything he could to earn their fare but he wouldn't hear of Alice working. He said she was too young, and it was too dangerous on the streets of Chicago.

"Here boy, reckon you deserved this." Jack threw wolf a smelly bone. He gave Alice a bowl of hot stew. "Don't lose the bowl, I have to take it back tomorrow. Got me a new job. Don't tell ma but I've become an expert at washing dishes. Paying me twenty-five cents a day too."

Alice didn't know how much it would cost for tickets to New York. She sat with her back to the brown case Mrs. Denton had packed their spare clothes in. Agatha sat beside her on the floor. Her stomach rumbled in appreciation of the delicious aroma coming from the dish. "Congratulations, Jack. How come you're not eating?"

Jack didn't meet her eyes. "I ate already. Anything happen today?"

Alice shook her head. It was pointless telling Jack about the footsteps, he'd only worry. He might insist on taking her to another orphanage. He'd threatened to do that when she wouldn't hear of him getting a job and leaving her in the hut alone. She ate a couple of mouthfuls, closing her eyes in bliss as the warm food calmed the hunger pains. She glanced at Jack to thank him only to catch him looking at her stew, a wistful expression in his eyes.

"Here, you eat it. I have a stomach pain."

She did too. Every time she thought of her father and whether he'd want her back, she felt ill. Jack ate so quickly, he barely gave himself a chance to swallow.

"You had nothing to eat did you?"

He flushed but didn't answer.

"Jack you have to be honest with me. How long will it take to earn our tickets if you can't work because you're ill? You will get sick if you don't eat."

He was thinner than she'd ever seen him. She knew he missed his Ma and her cooking. She did too. She didn't think twice about the Ackermans. Miss Lawlor told her Mrs. Ackerman would survive but would spend time in the hospital.

"If I was older and stronger, I'd get better work. I'm doing the best I can, Alice."

"I know you are. I just wish you'd agree to do what that hobo man said. The one who's seen the whole country without paying a penny on train fares."

Jack rolled his eyes.

"Jack, I'm serious. Why don't we try? What do we have to lose?"

"Our freedom?"

Alice hesitated. She knew they'd send her back to the orphanage or the Ackermans. But what would happen to Jack, he was older.

"If we're caught, I'll tell them I ran away, and you tried to stop me. You'll be a hero."

"Some hero, leaving you alone all day with only Wolf to mind you."

Wolf barked as if to protest.

"You said riding the rails was dangerous. Nobody will come near us if we take Wolf. Jack, I have to get back to New York."

Jack sighed. "You win. Never knew a girl go on so much."

"Thank you, Jack." She threw herself at him, knocking him over. He tickled her making her giggle.

"You're the best friend any girl could ask for, Jack Denton."

He gave her a funny look, mumbled something about going to wash up and left the hut. Wolf whined but didn't move. Alice glanced from the dog to the doorway and back again. What had she said to upset Jack?

* * *

Jack worked out the week so they could buy some food. He bought an old map for two pennies and they poured over this in the evenings, trying to plan the best route. Alice's heart hammered as she tried to remember the names of the stations she had visited on her way out west.

"We leave in the morning. Early. Wolf, do as you're told. Alice, you too. We can't afford any mistakes."

"Yes, Sir."

"Alice, I think you should cut your hair."

Alice shook her head. She'd spent the last three years trying to grow it out.

"It's better you look like a boy, not a girl."

"Why?"

Jack colored. "Just is."

"I'm not cutting my hair."

"We haven't even left yet, and you won't do as you're told. Cut your hair. They're looking for a boy and a girl. We need to act like brothers."

"Oh!" Alice knew he was right but hated his suggestion all the same. She didn't have scissors either.

"Can you use your knife?"

He nodded.

She cried, cuddling Agatha close, as the blonde tresses fell around her feet.

"It'll grow back. Even nicer than before." Jack muttered.

Alice didn't reply. When he finished, he produced a hat for her to wear. It smelled horrible but still she didn't protest. She had learned her lesson.

"Alice, I wouldn't do anything to hurt you, you know that. I just want to protect you. There are some things you can't understand, not at age nine."

She nodded. She didn't know what he was talking about but she knew he'd never hurt her. "How long do you think it will be until we are in New York?"

"About two weeks, maybe earlier if we're lucky. We have to avoid the guards and stay out of sight."

Butterflies flew around her stomach. Scared but excited too, she couldn't sleep that night.

The next morning, Jack woke her early. They ate a stale roll with a cup of hot water. Moving quickly but quietly, they hurried to the train tracks. Jack had identified the train they needed the night before. He helped Alice climb into one of the freight cars, Wolf followed by jumping in. Jack threw up their small bag of belongings before he jumped up and closed the door over. He didn't close it completely.

"Move back behind those goods. The guard might inspect the car and we don't want him to see us."

Alice did what he said, holding Wolf by the scruff of the neck. "Got to be silent, Wolf."

The dog seemed to understand as it wagged his tail but didn't bark. They settled, as comfortable as they could be in the confined space. Wolf chewed on his bone while Jack read a book. Alice stared into space day dreaming. Would New York have changed much since she left? Would Miss Baker welcome her back with open arms? She ran her fingers through what remained of her hair. What would her father think of her, especially as she looked like a boy?

CHAPTER 33

*A*lice soon tired of looking out at the view as they traveled the rails. If they came to a town, she and Jack hid in one of the dark corners keeping a tight grip on Wolf. Alice sensed Jack relaxing as they continued to travel unmolested. Her excitement grew as the miles passed by.

She woke up to Wolf growling. Putting her hand on his neck, she whispered "What is it? Jack?"

There was no answer. She jumped to her feet, but it was too dark to see Jack. He'd gone to look for food some time back. She must have fallen asleep. The train they'd been on, took a route away from New York so they'd jumped off the first chance they got. Jack apologizing for picking the wrong train, but Alice knew it wasn't his fault. They couldn't go up to a guard and ask them where the train was heading, could they?

"Who's there? Come out now and I won't hurt ya."

Wolf growled louder.

"Come on man, I can hear the dog. Best deal with me before I call the cops. Let's have a look at you?"

A lantern swung inside the boxcar as a man climbed in. Wolf pulled against Alice's grip but she couldn't let him attack. Not unless the man was a threat. His voice didn't sound angry.

"You alone, lad. You can't be over eight years old. What's an itty bitty little thing doing alone in a boxcar? You know how dangerous it can be out here?" The man came closer, holding his hand out to Wolf. "Hello boy, you're doing a great job of minding this lad. You hungry?"

Wolf sniffed the man's hand and then barked. Alice couldn't believe it.

"That's a mighty fine dog, you got there, Son. Part Wolf if I'm not mistaken. Got a name?"

"Al... Alex." Alice caught herself in time.

"Pleased to meet you, I'm Dessie. I'm a guard

on this train. Just checkin' it out as we head out in the morning. Where you off to?"

"Big City." Jack had warned her not to tell anyone where they were heading.

"Why are you traveling alone?"

"He isn't. He's with me. Wolf, here boy." Wolf ran to Jack's side. Jack held a stick as a weapon but it didn't seem to bother Dessie.

"Put the stick down lad. I ain't going to harm you or turn you in. It's a cold night out there. Want to share my fire?"

Jack stared at Dessie for a few seconds. "Why?"

"I'd like a bit of company. Gets lonesome out on a night like this. I used to ride the rails, before I turned respectable. It's no life for young un's particularly his age." Dessie pointed to Alice. "I got some stew going spare if you want to join me. Just follow me."

Alice moved to follow but a look from Jack halted her mid-stride. He shook his head.

"Thanks all the same Mister but we're moving on. We got new jobs waiting for us."

Jack pulled the brown case with one hand, Alice with the other and headed to the side of the boxcar. He jumped down, pulled Alice beside him and then reached for the case. Dessie handed it down to him. Wolf jumped.

"You take care of that youngster. If you're heading for New York, it's the last train on your right as you leave the yard. Good luck little fella."

Dessie jumped down from the car, took his lantern and walked away without looking back.

"What did you have to say no for? I'm starving."

"Come on Alice, we have to get out of here."

"No, I want to go after Dessie. He's nice."

"It could be a trap, Alice. We can't risk it. Come on. I got some bread for you."

Alice didn't think Dessie meant them any harm but Jack was older. Grumbling she tottered after him trying to keep up with his long strides. They spent the night in the open on the far side of the road nearest the depot. It was freezing. They couldn't light a fire for fear of being seen so they shared their bedroll. Jack slept with his back to her and Wolf slept on the other side, keeping Alice warm. Despite her fear of the dark, she fell asleep.

Jack woke her before daylight. "Come on, let's risk that train. Can't be any more dangerous than staying here. They'll spot us as soon as it gets light."

Alice yawned and stretched. She drank a little water and then shared some with Wolf. Jack picked up their bedrolls and carried the suitcase leaving Alice to carry Agatha. She thought their footsteps were loud when they approached the boxcars but Jack didn't stop moving. Nobody shouted out or lit a lantern. Jack put the case down and jumped up into a boxcar, he was soon back beside her. "Group of men already in there." He whispered.

They moved to the next boxcar and the next. On the last but one, Jack gave her a thumbs up and reached out to take the case and then to pull her by the arm up beside her. "Get comfortable. You should try to go back to sleep. I'll keep watch."

Alice didn't have time to move as Wolf growled and jumped out of the boxcar. Jack grabbed Alice to stop her going after the dog. They heard some men swearing as Wolf growled and snarled.

"Beat it over the head, stupid dog."

"I ain't getting closer to it, can't you see those teeth. They'd rip a man apart."

"Barney, I told ya to hit it. If you don't, I'll hit ya and leave you on the ground for his dinner."

Alice held her breath, praying silently. Please Wolf, don't get hurt. Come back to us.

Wolf yelped, then growled. Someone screamed. "Barney you get back here."

"Not on your life. He bit me. I probably got some disease. I'm off to get the guard. He'll shoot it."

Jack pulled Alice into his arms and held her steady. She tried to push him away, wanting to rescue Wolf, but he was stronger than she was. A whistle blew, and the train moved. Alice tried to scream but Jack held his hand over her mouth. She bit and kicked but to no avail. Only when they were out of the station did he release her.

"Why? You should have let me go to him. He's all I got."

"You got me. Wolf can look after himself. He'll be back." Jack didn't look at her but went to the edge of the boxcar staring out. The train picked up speed. Alice crawled to the space beside Jack, she didn't like being near the opening in case she fell out. She looked over his shoulder but couldn't see Wolf. Then Jack whistled and suddenly Wolf was running beside the train. Alice's heart hammered as the dog jumped. He barely made it, Jack grabbed the back of his neck and pulled him inside.

"Wolf, are you hurt?" She examined the dog from head to foot, he limped slightly.

Jack took over examining him. "Looks like he caught a belt on the back right leg. Hold still boy and let me see."

Jack pointed out the welt to Alice.

"My poor Wolf, how could that nasty man hurt you." Alice gathered the dog in her arms and let him lick her tears away.

At the next stop, Alice put both arms around Wolf to stop him jumping out. He whimpered, but she refused to let him go. She couldn't bear to lose him. Just as the train pulled out, a man swung himself into their boxcar. She stifled a scream. A jagged scar cut through the right hand side of his face.

"Evening folks. Don't mind me tagging along do ya?"

Wolf strained away from Alice.

"Let Wolf go." Jack hissed.

Wolf lunged at the man. The man whistled softly as he stood still. "That's a mighty big dog."

"He's a killer so you might as well hop on off the train."

"Can't do that, lad. At this speed, I'm likely to

lose a leg or an arm. I'll take my chances with the dog."

Wolf snarled. The man held out his hand, looking Wolf in the eyes. "Down, Wolf," Alice called out. Wolf glanced back at her and then sat down, his eyes trained on the man.

"Well trained too. You're a lovely boy aren't you?" The man held out his hand. Wolf sniffed it but didn't move closer. "What's your name kids?"

"Alex and Larry," Jack lied.

"Mine's Piper, not my real name but that's what they call me. Traveling far?"

Jack didn't answer. Piper shrugged his shoulders. "Not friendly are ya? But then I guess you got to be careful. Been riding the rails a long time. Seen a lot." Piper reached let his back fall to the floor. Alice noticed the tin cans he had attached to his belt. She wondered what they were for.

"Do you mind if I play a little? Takes my mind off the cold and hunger, for a while."

Jack shook his head.

Piper took out a harmonica and played several tunes. Alice listened intently letting the music wash over her. When Piper finished, Wolf howled.

"Now boy are you telling me to play again or are you glad I've finished."

Alice forgot Jack's warnings to stay quiet in company. "You play well, Mr. Piper."

"Why thankee little lady. I don't have a lot, but music doesn't cost nothing."

Jack glared at Alice.

"Don't be mad with her, lad. She's safe with me. You both are. Ain't you heard of the hobo code?"

They both shook their head.

"We have a duty to protect youngsters like ye. The good hobos that is. There are some dingbats you got to be wary of."

Jack repeated, "Dingbats?"

"Sorry, that's our word for some nasty men who travel the rails. They steal from whoever they come across. You can't trust them, not even with Californian blankets."

Alice looked to Jack to translate, but he shrugged his shoulders.

"Newspapers you sleep under, little lady. That's what we call Californian blankets."

Fascinated, Alice moved closer. "What do you work at Mr. Piper?"

"I'm a wood butcher. I can make almost anything from wood. I'd have my shop and sell the things I make if my face wasn't likely to scare off the customers."

Alice touched the back of her head. "How did you get burned? A river burned me."

"It did?"

His disbelieving tone annoyed her. She turned and pointed to the marks at the back of her scalp and neck.

"Gee, I'm sorry. I didn't think you could burn in water. My ma burned me."

Alice didn't know what to say.

"She gave me a belt. I was too small to stay standing, so I fell. The fire was behind me. She pulled me out again, in time."

"She wasn't a good Ma."

"No, Little Lady guess she wasn't. She dumped me at the hospital. Never came back. When I got better, they sent me to an orphanage. I didn't last long. Didn't like it much. I ran away and stayed with a family of ex-slaves. The wife, she tended my burns and the husband, he taught me how to work with my hands. Reckon they saved my life. The salve she used meant I got more movement back on my arm and leg. Good people they were."

"Why did you leave?"

"Trouble was brewing. It was after the civil war but some didn't take kindly to a family like that raising a boy like me. Moses, he got beaten up, and I knew I had to leave. I went back a few years later but heard they went up North. I never saw them again."

Alice wanted to hug the man, instead she wound her hands around her knees. "Can you play something else?"

"Sure little lady. What do you know?"

"Christmas songs. Silent Night?"

He smiled before he wiped his harmonica and hit a few bum notes. Alice closed her eyes, feeling Jack move closer to her. She held his hand as Piper played Silent Night. The notes rose around them and for once, in a long time, she didn't feel cold or hungry. Piper continued to play until Alice fell asleep. She woke up to hear him and Jack talking but fell back asleep before it registered what they were saying. Once more, she dreamed going home. Would New York be as wonderful as she remembered?

CHAPTER 34

◈

THE TRIANGLE FACTORY, MARCH 1910

Maria almost stumbled getting out of the elevator.

"Careful Miss Mezza," Joseph the operator called. "Don't want you turning on your ankle."

With a muttered thanks, Maria pulled her coat closer and exited the building. Tempted to visit the stores, she knew she was only postponing the inevitable. She had to face Mama's stony silence at some point.

She heard someone shout her name and looked up to find Frieda waving at her. Her friend was running down the street causing more than one person to stare at her.

. . .

"Frieda, what are you doing here?"

"I thought you'd like to come to tea. Don't worry, it's at Lily's house, not the Sanctuary. So your Mama and Rosa can't object."

Maria tried to smile, but it wasn't easy. She missed Papa more every day. She hated working in the Triangle and any hope of getting on better with Rosa had disappeared. Rosa blamed her for Papa's death. Mama too. It made for an uncomfortable living space.

"Please say you'll come, Maria. I want to check on Mr. Weber."

"Alice's father. Is he still staying with Lily?"

Frieda looked to the left to check the road was clear before they walked. "I don't think so. I think he found an apartment close by."

"Do you think Lily might have news of Alice?"

"I don't know but if you stop chatting and we walk, we'll soon find out."

Frieda poked her tongue out. Maria laughed. Her friend knew just how to amuse her. She linked arms and off they walked.

"How's things at the Triangle, Maria? You didn't exactly skip out of the place."

"Just the same as Sarah predicted. The cakes and music at lunch have disappeared. They lock the doors during the day and they search our bags every evening. I'm not sure what they think people will steal. Would you risk your job for a shirtwaist?"

Frieda rolled her eyes. "Harris and Blanck will never change. Have you thought about getting another job?"

"I've tried but nobody wants to hire an Italian with a reputation for striking. I'm lucky Anna took me on."

Frieda sighed. "That's my fault isn't it? I encouraged you to strike and to help in the Local 25. I didn't think of the consequences. I was selfish."

Maria turned on her friend. "You are the least selfish person I know. I made my own decisions. I'm nobody's puppet."

Frieda held her hands up in a gesture of surrender. Shame rushed through Maria. "Sorry Frieda, I don't know what's got into me. I get so mad all of the time."

"You're grieving, Maria. You lost a wonderful father."

Maria nodded, too choked to speak.

"In time, it will get easier. The day will come when you think of your father and smile. Not soon but it will come."

Maria hoped Frieda spoke the truth. She couldn't bear going home, looking at Papa's empty chair. If she was a man, she would run away.

"How is Patrick?" Maria asked. Frieda blushed but her eyes lit up in a smile.

"Working hard, between the hospital and his studies. He is almost qualified. The next exam is the big one. He wants to be a surgeon eventually, but he said he will take some time off studying to practice medicine."

The time flew by and they were soon standing outside Lily's house. Frieda knocked on the door which flew open.

"Frieda and Maria too, come in. We have news."

Caught up in Lily's excitement, they followed their host into the sitting room where a large fire burned in the grate. Maria glanced around her, loving the decor. Lily had good taste.

"Maria, please don't be shy. Cook made some tea, coffee and outdid herself with her muffins and pastries. Help yourself. Now, where are Charlie and Gustav?"

"Gustav is here?"

"He and Charlie hit it off straight away. Charlie got him a job in a small factory near here. Gustav has a new set of rooms too. He calls in here sometimes to check on news of Alice."

"Do you have any?"

"We had another letter from the teacher Miss Lawlor. Kathleen was right, the woman was trying to keep Alice safe. Alice had money for a ticket to New York and should have been here weeks ago. Miss Lawlor said Jack, the boy who is traveling with Alice is a sensible lad. We can't understand what happened. Why they haven't turned up. Have you heard anything?"

"No Lily. My friend, Sarah, knew Gustav from Little Germany. At least she knew him to see. She's told her friends and neighbors about Alice but nobody has seen anything. Sarah left me a note just yesterday."

"I wonder where Alice is? I hope she hasn't landed in trouble."

* * *

PIPER STAYED with Alice and Jack for days. He gave them tips on how to survive the trains and how to find food and shelter if they needed to leave one train and wait for another.

"You need to avoid the belly robbers and look for angels."

Alice laughed. "What?"

Piper rolled his eyes. "Belly robbers are the food joints serving small portions. Angels are housewives who invite you into their houses and give you a slap up meal. Angels love children but some of them are real do gooders. They will have you at the local orphanage before you know what hit you."

Alice shivered. Jack put his arm around her. "You aren't going to another orphanage. I won't let that happen."

Piper seemed to realize his error. "Course not. Between Jack and Wolf, you have the best protection you could get."

"Why don't you come to New York with us too, Mr. Piper."

"Don't do well with big cities, Little lady. Can't breathe with all those people. The tall buildings give me nightmares. Prefer the outlying farms myself. Like animals I do. More trustworthy than people and they don't mind my face."

Alice reached out to touch his face. "I like your face, Mr. Piper. I think an angel sent you to look after us."

The old man stared at a point above her face. She wished she could make the sadness in his eyes disappear.

"What will you do with Wolf when you get to New York, little lady?"

Alice didn't know. She looked to Jack, but he didn't answer.

"My father will let me keep him."

The man held out his hand. Alice took it.

"I know you believe that Little Lady but from what you've told me, there's no guarantee your father could do that. He might live in one of those apartment places that don't allow animals. Lots of people in New York hate wolves. They had a bad reputation."

"I can't lose him." Alice's lip wobbled.

"You love him, I can see that. But you don't want Wolf to get hurt or worse do you?"

Alice shook her head.

"There was a time when a dogcatcher could earn a lot of dollars for catching a beauty like Wolf. You don't want to risk that."

Alice grabbed Wolf, causing the dog to whimper. "You just want my dog. He's mine not yours."

"Alice, don't be silly. Piper is telling the truth. We can't risk bringing Wolf to the city."

"I won't leave him. I won't."

"But you said you loved him. Are you going to be the reason he dies?" Jack whispered, stroking the dog on the head.

"No, but... I don't want to lose him."

"I know you don't, Little Lady but you can't take him with you. Wouldn't be fair to your family or to Wolf."

"Jack?" Alice bedded him to make the decision.

"Piper, would you take Wolf and look after him for Alice?"

Piper nodded slowly. "I love all God's creatures. I wouldn't let nothing happen to him."

Alice's tears flowed down her face. Wolf licked them, his paws on her chest.

She protested "Wolf, you need a bath."

Wolf just licked her more making them all laugh.

"I'm sorry for being horrible to you Mr. Piper."

"I understand Little Lady. You love Wolf as much as he loves you." Piper glanced out the moving train. "You got another day or so to say your goodbyes and then I best be leaving. You should be in New York in three days."

Alice closed her eyes. Three days and she'd be home. After all this time, she hoped it would be everything she dreamed about. Her hand went to her hair.

"Little lady, your father be a lucky man to have a girl like you."

All reservations forgotten, Alice threw herself into the man's arms and squeezed him tight. "I hope he feels the same way, Mr. Piper. I hope he's as nice as you."

She felt his tears on her hair. Together they cried for a little while. Alice nodded off to sleep as night fell, still wrapped in Mr. Piper's arms. She dreamed of New York.

CHAPTER 35

Maria strode out of the lift as it reached the 9th floor thinking it was the 10th. She didn't notice her mistake until she saw the cutters. Tired after yet another argument at home, she hadn't been paying attention. She didn't know what time she'd got to bed. Mama and Rosa had argued again over Paulo Greco. Mama expected Maria to support her. Rosa wanted to get married and Mama felt it was too soon after Papa's death. She could hear her Mama screaming how disrespectful it was. Rosa had yelled back like a fishwife. Maria pushed her hair back from her eyes "That's better, you can see your pretty eyes now."

She blushed as she caught his admiring gaze.

Conrad Schneider, a way too attractive man stood hands on his hips as he stared back at her.

"You better concentrate on your cutting. Otherwise the boss will have words with you."

"He can talk all he likes, but he knows there's no better cutter in the whole of New York."

She tried not to laugh as his eyes twinkled. "Self-praise is no praise," she retorted.

"Come closer and I'll show you."

She moved nearer ignoring the ribald comments from the other cutters. What these men did fascinated her. She knew they earned up to twenty dollars per week – a fortune compared to the pitiful amounts they paid the seamstresses. All cutters were men but maybe she could be the first woman to do the job.

"See this? We put the fabric in layers on the table. Then we put the paper patterns on the very top. The secret is to assemble these pieces as close together to prevent waste."

Mesmerized now, Maria forgot about the other cutters. She peered over the table watching Conrad lay out the paper pattern for both sleeves, the collar, cuffs, and the back and front.

"If you put them like this?" Conrad rearranged the papers, swopping one sleeve for the back. "You will cut fewer pieces. Fewer pieces means less profit, and the boss has a tantrum. Seeing how best to lay each piece on the material is key to being a successful cutter."

"You teaching a lass how to do our job, Schneider? Waste of time, mate. They'll never let a woman be a cutter. Pure stupid they are."

Maria ignored the English man and at first thought Conrad had too, but she saw his eyes narrowing. But he didn't pretend he heard. He continued his lesson.

"Only when you are sure of your placements, do you cut. Measure twice and cut once my mam used to say to me."

Maria couldn't hide her disbelief. "Your mother was a cutter?"

"Nah, not in the way you mean. She was a dressmaker back in Ireland. She sewed for the gentry up at the big house. Was good with her hands was my mam. She showed me everything she knew. It was only me and her." For a second, a sorrowful expression clouded his eyes.

Schneider wasn't an Irish name, yet he spoke with an accent. His next words distracted Maria.

"With these new cutting machines, we can cut larger amounts of cloth, so you have to be cautious as more room for error. Still there is always waste." Conrad indicated the big boxes full of cloth remnants. "The boss sells that onto a friend. He will collect it every couple of months and sell it on at a profit. Nothing gets wasted really, not at the Triangle."

Maria glanced at the clock. Another few minutes and she had to be at her machine.

"Have you worked here long?"

"You mean you haven't noticed me before?" He was flirting, and she enjoyed it. But it wasn't seemly to let a man think you were available.

"I'm too busy to notice anyone. Thanks for the lesson. I have to get on." She walked off without glancing back although it took every ounce of restraint not to. Was he looking at her or had his eye moved onto another young lady? Maria Mezza, what are you thinking? Mama would spend hours praying and light candles for her soul, if she started walking out with an Irish man. Papa, oh my goodness what was she doing thinking about a man. Papa wasn't long dead and here she was giggling like a schoolgirl.

She closed her eyes and murmured a plea for forgiveness. The whistle blew, the machines started rumbling and all thoughts of anything other than the seam she had to stitch flew from her mind.

Rosa waited for her when the day was over. Her sister pinched her hard.

"What was that for?"

"Your name is all over the factory. What were you doing flirting with a cutter, an Irishman of all things?"

"I wasn't flirting," Maria lied. "Conrad was teaching me about his job. It's fascinating. I want to be a cutter one day."

Rosa stared at her and then burst out laughing. "You? A cutter? You might as well wish to become a priest. Cutters are always men. No factory will employ a girl as a cutter. You need to accept your place in life Maria, or you will be very unhappy. I don't know what I will tell Mama."

"Why do you have to tell her anything?" Maria hated begging her sister, but she didn't need a lecture from Mama about her morals or worse to look for a match for her. In the old country she would be engaged if not married by now. Some of her friends in the tenements already had one child with another on the way. Those girls looked older than she did, worried about making ends meet. That wasn't the life she wanted.

***

THE NEXT DAY she spotted Conrad at the lift. She caught him glance in her direction, but she pretended not to see him. She didn't want to upset Rosa and if her sister was correct about the gossip, maybe the women would pick on someone else. But she hadn't banked on Conrad's determination to speak to her. When they broke for their thirty-minute lunch break, Conrad came and stood by her machine. He handed her an apple.

"Yours I believe. You dropped it as you ran in this morning."

Her cheeks grew hot as she looked at his face, both knowing she hadn't seen the apple till now. She glanced around quickly but her colleagues seemed caught up in their own lunches.

"Thank you." She took a bite from the apple, laughing as some juice dribbled down her chin. He smiled, lifting his hand as if to wipe the juice away but at the last minute dropping it as if he remembered where they were.

"I wondered if you would let me walk you home this evening?" he whispered as he reached down to put something in the bin.

Her heart beat faster as she wanted to say yes

but what about Rosa? Tomorrow Rosa was meeting Paulo.

"It's not possible tonight but I'm free tomorrow as Rosa has plans. Just don't tell anyone."

He put a finger up to his lips and left. She stared down at her machine for fear of catching one of the other girls looking at her. She would light up like a candle. She couldn't let that happen, but neither was she going to stand Conrad up. They could take a walk around the market first and she would just say they left work at the same time. The back to work whistle soon put a stop to her rambling thoughts.

CHAPTER 36

The next night, Conrad waited for her in Washington Park as they'd agreed. Maria had smiled tightly when Paulo collected Rosa outside the factory door. She'd promised to tell Mama they'd been out shopping. It was true too, they'd both gone shopping just not with each other.

She spotted Conrad standing near a tree. He was so very attractive. Not exactly handsome but the way his hair kept falling over his eyes was endearing. He had a lovely smile too.

"I thought you'd changed your mind and weren't coming." The look he gave her made her blush.

"I had to wait with my sister Rosa. Paulo, that's her fiancé he was late."

"Don't like him much do you?"

"He's all right. I don't really know him. He's a Greco." She waited to see if the name meant anything to Conrad, but it didn't appear to. She prompted, "The Greco name is well known in Sicily."

"You mean like everyone's name is Paddy or Bridget in Ireland?"

He had a lovely smile.

"No, not like that exactly. The Greco's provide protection amongst other things."

He stopped walking. "You mean he's mafia?"

"Shush," Maria glanced around them. "You don't call them that, at least not out loud. The correct term is Costa Nostra."

"Whatever you call them, what's your sister doing going out with one of them. She said your mother wouldn't like you meeting me yet she's with a…"

Maria cut him off. "What do you know about Mama? Have you been talking to Rosa? You have, haven't you?"

"Yes but not out of choice. She warned me off. She told me not to meet you tonight. But I wasn't about to let you stand in the park waiting for me."

Maria twisted her hands, if she got a hold of

Rosa now, she would wring her neck. How dare she?

"Maria, I did the right thing didn't I? Only you look so mad."

"I am furious but not at you. When will Rosa realize I make my own decisions? It's bad enough I have to work at the Triangle but who I talk to is my business. I will kill her."

Conrad's burst of laughter distracted her.

Hands on her hips, she waited for him to explain but he only laughed more. Finally, she gave in and asked, "What's so funny?"

"You are. I knew Italian girls were quick-tempered, but you must hold the record. Do you always get so hot and bothered?"

He made a funny face and Maria giggled. "No, not usually. Actually, Rosa is the one with the temper."

"Jeez remind me never to get on her bad side."

She could see he was joking, and it felt nice. She didn't have much experience with men apart from a few Italians boys who'd walked her home from the church in full view of her parents. Sons of her parents' friends. Not since Papa had died. And never anybody who made her feel like Conrad did when he looked at her.

"So now you met my sister, tell me about your family? Do you have sisters?"

"No, I was an only child."

"That's surprising. I heard Irish people had huge families." She smiled to show him she was joking too.

"They do, but my father died soon after I was born."

"I put my foot in it didn't I? Sorry."

"Don't be. You weren't to know. He was killed at work. Mam didn't look at anyone else not for lack of opportunities. She was a good-looking woman like you." He glanced at her, but she wouldn't meet his eyes. She'd only turn bright red, but it was nice to think he found her attractive too. Rosa was the beauty in the family.

"Your surname isn't Irish though is it?" she asked as they walked.

"Father was German. He and my mother met at Ellis Island. Mam said it was love at first sight. It must have been as marriages between a Lutheran and a Roman Catholic are not what you call common."

"Lutheran?" She'd never heard of that place.

"He was what you would call protestant. As in Martin Luther."

Maria nodded wondering what religion he had grown up in. If he was catholic, her mother would be slightly more welcoming.

"Mam brought me up in her church once Father died. The priest, he didn't recognize their wedding, but Mam said going to church reminded her of her home back in Ireland. She always wanted to go back, but it wasn't to be."

"She's dead?"

"Ten years now. She died from consumption. She got it working in a sweatshop our sort used to work in. No cure for TB. So that left me."

He had to be about twenty now, so he'd been young when she died.

"An aunt, my father's sister took me in for a while, but I left on my fourteenth birthday. We had what you might call differing views. She hated the Irish with a passion."

"How did you survive?" Maria couldn't imagine not having her family around her. She thought when Papa died, things might change. But Mama worked even harder to keep them together. When Benito or rather his wife had suggested sending the younger girls away to an orphanage, Mama had thrown them out of the house and wouldn't speak to them for a week. Mama and

Rosa might drive her nuts but at least they were always there.

"I worked hard and stayed out of trouble, most of the time. Then I met Mr. Rosen. He was a tailor looking for an apprentice. Mam had taught me how to cut cloth and sew a seam. Mr. Rosen took pity on me. Said I reminded him of his son. So, he took me on, trained me and here I am."

"Does he work at the Triangle too?" She knew a few Rosens but only women.

Conrad laughed. "Mr. Rosen? Not likely. He'd have pushed Harris out the window by now. No, he's gone out to California. Said he wanted to spend the rest of his days in the sun. Wanted me to go with him too."

Maria's breath caught. Conrad had almost gone to California. "You didn't fancy the sun?"

"I did, I still do. But I wanted to make my way. I promised Mam I'd go to see where she grew up, back in Ireland. See the big house she worked at, the village where her house was. She wanted me to find her family. As she was dying, she thought they'd forgive her for marrying a non-Catholic. I wrote to them, but nobody wrote back so I guess they weren't too forgiving. Funny how people hold on to hate isn't it?"

"Mama is like that, Rosa too if I am honest. They hate people they don't even know. Papa was slightly better, he tried…" her breath caught. It was still so painful talking about Papa.

"Your Papa?"

"He died just before I came to work at the Triangle."

"I'm sorry. I wish I'd met him. Did he like Germans? Rosa certainly doesn't like us."

Maria didn't answer the question. "Is that what you think of yourself as being? German? I just thought as you speak with an Irish accent you would be Irish."

"Me? I'm a true American."

They continued chatting as they walked around the different barrows, each stall holder shouting out their wares. Conrad bought her a pretzel and a hot drink.

"Is it that late? Mama will kill me. I have to get home. Sorry."

"Don't be. The time flew past." He walked her home only stopping when she suggested it wasn't a good idea for Mama or their neighbors to see them together. "I think you should leave me here. My apartment is just over there." She pointed in the general direction.

"I'd rather see you safely home."

"Thank you, but here is fine." Her neighbors might see her and report her to Mama. "Please, Conrad, my family can be difficult."

He turned to face her, still holding her hand.

"I really enjoyed tonight Maria. I hope you will come out again with me."

"I would like that."

He brushed the hair back from her eyes, his gaze locking with hers. "I'd like that too." His gaze dropped to her lips before moving back to her eyes. He lowered his head and gently brushed her cheek with his lips.

"I'll see you Monday morning, bright and early."

She could barely speak. Her first kiss. Not a real one but he'd kissed her face. She didn't remember walking home. Only when the door closed and Mama demanded to know where Rosa was, did she come back down to earth.

CHAPTER 37

Jack put his arm around Alice as they waved goodbye to Piper and Wolf. Tears streamed down everyone's faces. Even Wolf howled. Alice pushed him away when he tried to stay with them.

"Go with Mr. Piper, Wolf. He'll look after you. Now go." Don't forget me but she couldn't say those words aloud. She watched until the two of them disappeared into the distance.

Jack tried to cheer her up but nothing worked. Eventually, he gave up, and they pulled into New York in silence. Jack jumped off the freight car, looked around and only when he deemed it safe, did he help Alice down. The battered suitcase came last.

Alice cuddled Agatha as she looked around with

interest. She hadn't remembered how bad the station smelled or the volume of people passing by. She edged closer to Jack. He held tight to her hand.

Alice remembered bits and pieces about Little Germany. She could see her mother's face now, her blonde hair flowing across her shoulders when at home, secured in a bun when they took a walk.

"Jack, how long will it be before we get to Little Germany?"

"A while, Alice. I think we should go to Miss Lawlor's friends first. She's bound to have written them to expect us. They must be frantic."

"After I find my father, Jack."

"Alice, we've spoken about this. What if your father isn't there anymore?"

"He will be. I'll recognize where we live. I can see it now my memory has returned. I bet Eliza never thought her beating me would help me."

Jack scowled at the memory but didn't reply. He kept looking around as he held her hand tighter. They had to be careful where they walked due to the mounds of horse dung on the roads. They tried to stick to the main streets heading Pipers warning to avoid back streets or large tenements due to the gangs. They spotted children their own age on every street corner. Some were playing, most were trying to earn a living. Some were selling wood or bits and pieces. Alice didn't know what others were selling as they just stood there, their pale white faces drawn in hunger. She ignored her own hunger pangs. Their money had run out and Jack didn't want to leave her alone to get a job.

On they walked, hiding in stores if they saw an officer on patrol. Jack didn't trust the police. They jumped on a tram, heading to Little Germany. The tram terminated before it reached its final destination, some fault with the lines or something. Alice didn't care, they were almost there. She would be home soon.

Things were going well until they turned into a street. An officer glanced their way, saw Jack stop and turn into the store. Instead of ignoring them, the officer waited for them to come out again.

"What are you two up to?"

"Nothing sir, just going home."

"Where's home?" The officer asked, suspicion all over his face.

"Little Germany," Alice responded just as Jack said Brooklyn.

"So which is it? What's a girl your age doing

with a lad like him?" The officer directed the question to Alice but kept his eyes on Jack.

"He's my friend."

The officer's eyes widened. The suspicion deepened. "What have you got in the case?"

Jack held the officer's gaze. "Clothes."

The officer cuffed him across the head taking both children by surprise.

"You mind your manners and don't cheek me boy. Why would a pair of kids need a case of clothes unless they're runways? Out with it, what orphanage are you from?"

Jack exchanged a glance with Alice, moving his eyes left.

She waited for his sign, her mouth dry.

"I asked you a question," the policeman came closer.

"Run," Jack shouted as he kicked the officer on the leg, grabbed Alice's hand and almost swung her off her feet. They took off down a street, the officer in close pursuit. They ran and ran but Alice couldn't keep going. Fighting for breath, she had to stop. Jack surveyed their surroundings. "Down here. I will come back for you but I have to lose the officer."

"Don't leave me Jack."

"I have to. You'll be safe here. Keep your head down. I will be back in an hour at most."

Before she could protest, he'd run off. She bent down beside the case, praying he would get back fast. Nobody bothered her, he'd chosen the spot well. She didn't know what time it was. Then she heard Jack. She jumped up and back down again as she spotted him being dragged along the street, a different police officer holding him by the ear.

"Nobody innocent runs from us, son. We'll soon find out what you were up to."

CHAPTER 38

Torn between giving herself up and finding her father, she wavered. Jack didn't look in her direction which made her think he didn't want her discovered. She waited until she couldn't see him anymore and then started walking as fast as she could, the battered suitcase in one hand, Agatha in the other.

"Want a hand with your case?" A boy asked her. She shook her head.

"Are you sure? You don't look strong enough."

"No, my brother he's just behind me. He'll carry it soon. Thanks though."

The boy glanced around. Alice stared at a tall boy some distance back and waved. The boy returned the wave, so the youngster ran off.

Alice almost skipped as she recognized the street. Her mother used to bring her here to get ice cream. She remembered the shops. There was the butcher, she'd always hated the smell. There was the barber where her father had gone to get his hair cut. Various carts and stalls sold things on the street. She remembered there being more people but perhaps that was a trick of her memory.

Her home was around the next corner. She picked up her pace, dragging the suitcase. She would have dumped it only it held Jack's favorite book. She couldn't lose that not after everything he had done. She prayed he would be safe but policemen were kind to children. Weren't they?

She turned the corner and stared in disbelief at the scene in front of her. The whole area was deserted, the buildings falling down. She could make out the insides of some apartments, the walls at the front had been torn down.

"Hey kid, you shouldn't be down here. Not safe, it ain't. They're supposed to knock those buildings and build a factory but they got delayed with the strike. They could topple any minute." The man wheezed but despite that he lit a new cigarette from the one he was smoking. "You alone? You're young ain't you? Where's your mama?"

"Dead." Alice responded shortly. "Papa's coming behind me, he's pushing a big car filled with things. We're supposed to be meeting friends here shortly."

"You're moving into Little Germany? Good luck, girl. You'll need it. Most folks like you have left." The man went off, smoking and wheezing leaving Alice alone. Out of breath, and terrified, she shook as she put the case on the ground and almost fell down on top of it. What was she going to do now?

* * *

Frieda opened the door to the loud knocking. A police officer marched in, closely followed by another handcuffed to a young boy. The boy's bruised face took her by surprise. She didn't challenge the officers.

"Frieda, who's making such a… What is the meaning of this? How dare you invade this property?" Kathleen drew herself up to her full height. The police officers didn't take any notice.

"This boy says he has a message for Miss Lily or Miss Kathleen. He won't talk to no-one else."

"How did he hurt his face?" Frieda demanded

at the same time as Kathleen said, "I'm Mrs. Kathleen Green. Take those cuffs off that boy at once. Frieda, can you get some clean water and attend to him?"

The officer snarled, "Nobody's touching him."

"Officer perhaps you've heard of my husband, Dr. Richard Green? This young lady is one of his medical students and she will examine the child. You will remove the cuffs or I shall place a call to Inspector Griffin." Kathleen stared the officer down. "I see by your expression, his name is familiar."

The officer didn't respond but pulled the boy closer and released the cuffs.

"Thanks Missus. They hurt. I need your help. My name is Jack and Miss Lawlor said I.."

"Jack Denton. Thank goodness you've turned up. We're going out of our minds with worry. But where is Alice?"

"I don't know." The boy looked so miserable Frieda wanted to give him a hug. Instead, Kathleen moved closer to him.

"Jack, start from the beginning. Where did you see Alice last?"

The whole sorry tale about being chased by the police, him trying to protect Alice and in the process losing her came tumbling out. Mesmerized, Frieda couldn't move. She listened to the tale with growing horror. What had become of a young innocent child alone on the streets?

"Cook, there you are. Can you please take care of this young man? If one of these....officers... make a move near him, you ring Inspector Griffin. Thank goodness Lily got a telephone installed in her home as well as here. I'll ring her. She'll find Gustav and Charlie. Frieda, go outside and hail a cab but wait for me. You!"

The more junior police officer, given he was looking sheepish, jumped as Kathleen pointed at him. "Go to the local police station and tell them you need a search party."

"Me?"

"Yes you. While you are there put a call into Inspector Griffin and tell him Kathleen Green needs him in Little Germany. Now move."

The police officer nearly fell over his own feet as he raced out the door.

"Jack, you sit by the fire and get warm. We will be back as soon as we can."

The senior police officer responded. "Thanks kindly Missus, it's a cold night out there."

"The invitation was for Jack alone. You can sit

over there. This is a woman and children's sanctuary. You aren't welcome here."

The officer scowled but Frieda caught the triumphant smile on Jack's face before the worry took over once more.

Kathleen kept speaking. "Jack, we will find her. Have faith. We found her father and he will help us look."

"You did? Does he want her?"

"Yes, very much so."

Jack almost fell into the chair by the fire and by the time they were leaving, was fast asleep. "The poor boy, what age is he? Thirteen or fourteen? So much responsibility at such a young age."

Frieda didn't comment. Kathleen knew children grew up fast in their line of work. A few of the women from the Sanctuary came with them to join the search while the rest stayed behind to hold the fort. The cab didn't take long but Lily, Charlie and Gustav were waiting on the street, Alice had last been seen.

Kathleen paid the cab driver before saying, "Jack lost Alice when the police arrested him, he thinks she made her way to Little Germany. She is dying to see her father."

"My poor Alice, please let nothing happen to her. It's so cold and dark. She must be terrified."

"She's a strong young lady, Mr. Weber. Where do you think she might have gone?" Kathleen asked.

"To our old house but it's torn down now. It's cold so maybe the stores on the main street. To keep warm?"

Frieda agreed, and they marched off in that direction. More people joined the search, reuniting a victim of the General Slocum with her father bringing back many memories.

"We'll find her soon, Gustav."

"Ya, we must hope so." Gustav lapsed into German as he said a prayer. Frieda followed suit. She could almost see her Vati, smiling down at her, his arm around Muttis's shoulder with the children standing in front. She blinked away the vision of her family as she followed Gustav.

CHAPTER 39

Darkness fell and still Alice couldn't walk. It was like they glued her to the ground. She couldn't find the energy to move her legs. She was all alone and she couldn't remember the address of Miss Lawlor's friends. She wanted to ask a policeman to help her but after seeing how they treated Jack; fear stopped her. She hugged Agatha close as the cold ground seeped through her clothes. She climbed on top of the case as it was slightly warmer.

There was nobody around which was comforting and scary at the same time. She heard leaves rustling, was it the wind or rats? A cat screeched followed by a barking dog. In the distance she could hear bells - was it a fire engine or an ambulance? She closed her eyes remembering her past, the smell of smoke, the water, the bells on the ambulance. It had taken her away from the river to the hospital. She could feel the terror of riding with strangers looking after her. They wouldn't tell her where Mutti was. She screamed as they rubbed something on her head after they cut her hair.

She held her hand to her head, her hair was once again short. A tear escaped. This wasn't what she had imagined. The New York she'd daydreamed about through those horrible times with the Ackermans didn't exist. This place was full of scary people and places, she couldn't trust anyone. She longed for Jack or Miss Lawlor. She shouldn't have let Mr. Piper take Wolf. But then the policeman would have taken Wolf and maybe now he'd be dead. At least Wolf was still alive and happy. She closed her eyes, trying not to, but she was so tired.

All the traveling, the hopes and dreams were for nothing. There was nobody here for her. They had all left her alone.

In her dream, she could hear someone shouting her name. The sounds echoed around her, like a thousand people were screaming her name. Shaking her head, she tried to get out of the nightmare but it continued.

Someone was shouting, "Alice, Alice, where are you?"

She was here. She tried to call out but her voice wouldn't work. It croaked rather like the bullfrog Jacob had kept as a pet. She tried again, but it was no use. Shivering, she wrapped her arms around her. Agatha slipped to the ground, but she didn't have the energy to pick her up. When she closed her eyes, her body felt funny. Like it wanted to slip away. But she had nowhere left to go.

* * *

"Quick, look there she is."

Frieda turned in time to see Gustav racing across a street toward a bundle lying on the road. She followed on his heels as he almost staggered to a stop.

"Alice, wake up. Wake up." He picked up the child but her arms dangled lifeless by his side. Frieda rushed forward.

"Let me see her." She pushed her hand under the child's clothes, her hands and feet were freezing yet she was burning up with fever.

Gustav cried out, "she's dead isn't she? I've lost her again."

"No. Shush. She's alive but barely. We have to get her to the hospital. Gustav lie her on my coat." Frieda took off her coat and lay it on the ground. "Gustav lay her down. Run for a cab. I will help her breathe."

Frieda shouted at him to do what he was bid and finally he reacted. She pushed aside the child's clothes to check her heart was beating. Then she wrapped her up in a bundle before she briskly worked on her legs and arms to get the circulation moving. She prayed the cab would hurry. The word spread. Kathleen arrived at the same time as the cab, took one glance at Alice and gave Frieda her coat.

"Take her to the hospital. We'll go back to the Sanctuary and wait there for news. God speed."

Frieda gave the child to Gustav to carry to the waiting cab. She gave the cab driver instructions to ride like his life depended on it. She wasn't losing this child not after everything Alice had endured.

Richard Green greeted her on the hospital steps. "Kathleen phoned me. How is she?"

"Frozen but her temperature is sky high. I can't see any sign of infection but the light was bad. She has several injures in various stages of healing."

Frieda persuaded Gustav to give Alice into

Richard's care. "He is the best doctor in New York. Trust him."

Gustav kissed Alice's cheek before handing her over. Frieda grabbed Gustav's arm to support him as it looked like his legs would give way.

"Let me help you," Patrick added. She hadn't even noticed he was there.

"Thank you. I should go help your father."

Patrick held Gustav with his arm around the man's waist and led him to a chair.

"Frieda, you should sit down and have a hot drink. This is no weather to be out without a coat."

Frieda glanced down at her shirtwaist. "I gave mine to Alice. Your mom gave me her coat but Alice was shivering so we wrapped her up in it as well."

"Stay here, I will get the drinks. Don't leave your patient." Patrick indicated Gustav.

Frieda was freezing. She sat beside Gustav and rubbed his hands trying to get some feeling back into her own at the same time. Patrick arrived back with hot sweet tea and some blankets. "I will find out what is happening."

The minutes moved slower than seconds as Frieda stared at the clock. Gustav was incapable of conversation, he stayed silent and barely moved.

This couldn't be how the story ended. Not after everything.

Maria rushed to them.

"Frieda, there you are. We heard the news and came straight away."

"Hello Gustav. I'm Conrad from the Triangle. I recognize you from taking the elevator." The man with Maria greeted Gustav.

The older man blinked before he started sobbing. "Alice, my Alice. I failed her again."

Conrad spoke, his tone firm. "You did no such thing. You found her, Gustav and now she is being cared for by the best people. Don't give up now."

Frieda glanced at Maria but her friend shrugged her shoulders.

Gustav shuddered and then found his voice.

"Conrad, I should have tried harder. When I first found out the orphanage had sent her West, I should have gone after her. They wouldn't tell me where she was. I didn't mean for her to go forever. Just for a while until I could earn some money to pay someone to look after her. There was no one to take her. Our friends, our family all died on that boat."

Frieda's tears overflowed, she kept brushing them away but they wouldn't stop. The poor man. She needed a minute alone to compose herself. She stood up.

"I will see what I can find out, Gustav. You wait here with our friends."

"I'm coming with you. Conrad will look after Gustav." Maria declared, her tone telling Frieda it would be pointless to argue.

Maria took Frieda's arm in hers. "You look done in. Have you had anything to eat? Where is your coat?"

"I gave it to Alice. Conrad? He is your new friend?"

She saw the heat rise in Maria's cheeks. "He seems lovely." Maria didn't respond. Frieda led them to the wards.

"Patrick, how is she?"

"Doing better. Dad said I was to get you and her father. He thinks her seeing Gustav will help. And she keeps asking for Jack."

"Poor lad is back in the Sanctuary with your mother. The police brought him in with handcuffs, I thought Kathleen would explode." Frieda described the scene to her two friends.

"Good on Mother. Wouldn't like to be the one explaining why the boy was treated so badly."

"I thought your mother was going to take the bible message an eye for an eye a bit too literally."

Patrick smiled as he reached out to feel her forehead. She heated, no doubt sending her temperature sky high.

"You need to be more careful, darling Frieda." He called her darling. She knew she was blushing and smiling like an idiot but she didn't care.

"The hospital can't afford to lose good doctors."

She fell back to earth with a bump. That's all she was to him. A fellow doctor. She waved him off when he said he'd go back for Gustav if she wanted to go into Alice. Maria said she'd wait outside the ward, not wanting to overcrowd the poor girl.

Frieda walked on tippy toes as Alice appeared to be sleeping. Richard Green stood by her bed, listening to her chest. He smiled when he saw her.

"Her chest is clear. She has a slight chill but nothing a week's worth of good food and some decent accommodation won't cure. She was lucky."

Frieda glanced at the child, seeing the marks on her arms. The same as those she had spotted on her legs.

Lucky? He caught her reaction. "Frieda, she's safe now. Nothing and nobody will hurt her now."

Frieda tried to smile but found she couldn't. The tears threatened again. Why would anyone hurt a defenseless child so badly? She'd never understand not till the day she died.

Patrick arrived back, partially supporting Gustav by the arm. Frieda suspected the man was half starved She wondered what type of job he had told Lily and Charlie he had because he evidently didn't earn enough to eat properly.

"Alice, she will be fine?" he asked, his German accent stronger than ever.

"Yes, Mr. Weber, your daughter is a strong young lady. She needs proper care, decent food and lodgings but she will make a full recovery."

"Thank you, so much. All of you." Gustav pulled free of Patrick and sat on the chair near the bed, holding Alice's hand.

"Alice, it's Papa. You're home. You're safe now. Papa won't let anyone take you away."

* * *

ALICE COULD HEAR a voice talking to her, it sounded familiar yet it wasn't Jack. She opened her eyes, closing them again as the bright light hurt them.

A woman spoke softly. "Alice, try again. I turned off the lamp."

Alice opened her eyes and there he was. "Papa? You're here? Did I die? Am I in heaven?"

"Not heaven, but New York. You're home."

"Papa, I made it. Jack said I would. I wish he was here too."

"Jack can visit you later, he's with my friends. They have given him a bath, some clothes and some food. My name is Frieda, I was on the General Slocum too. I know what you've been through. Your father has worked so hard to find you. He loves you, sweetheart."

"He does? But Papa, my hair?" Alice looked at her father, her hand on her hair.

Gustave looked confused as he glanced at Frieda then back at Alice.

"What about your hair?"

Alice wailed, "I look like a boy."

Everyone burst out laughing as the child protested it wasn't funny.

Gustav wiped his eyes on his sleeve. "After everything, you think your hair could change how I feel. You could be bald and I wouldn't care. You are my Alice, home at last. Do you want this with you?"

In his hand he held Agatha. She grabbed her. "That's Agatha, my doll."

"Yes, my dearest child. Mutti made it for you when we found out we were having a new baby. She thought you would like something of your own."

"I knew it. I told Miss Baker my mother had made her for me. Agatha kept me company Papa, and she helped me get back to you. Wolf too."

CHAPTER 40

Frieda and Patrick took a cab back to the Sanctuary. Richard Green insisted on admitting Gustav to the hospital too. He was running a slight fever, besides being severely underweight. Gustav admitted he'd paid some people to find Alice. He never saw them again.

"How can people take advantage of someone like Gustav? Didn't he lose enough in the fire without those, those men stealing his money?"

"We know there are people like that all over the country not just in New York. Look at Alice. What type of man would beat a child like that?"

"What kind of woman would stand by and watch? I will go down to the Orphan Society offices and make a huge fuss. They should take more care about the people they accept to adopt or foster children."

"Frieda, leave the Orphan Society to Mother and Lily. You look exhausted and you have exams coming up. They must be your priority. Only when you are qualified, can you do more to help people like Gustav, Alice and all the others who need you."

Frieda pushed her bangs out of her eyes, exhaustion seeping into every bone of her body.

"Are you listening to me, Frieda? You can't work alone. You don't have to. You have a whole family who care about you."

She glanced at him under her eyelashes. Was that how he saw her? A member of his family, like a sister or cousin or something. Sighing, she closed her eyes. She couldn't think about stuff like that now.

* * *

"Thank goodness you are back. I have a rather impatient young man waiting for you. He wants to go to the hospital. I've told him it's too late and they won't let him in but boy is he being stubborn?"

Patrick said, "A match for you Lily? I'd never have believed it."

Lily rolled her eyes, took Frieda's arm and peppered her with questions about Alice and Gustav as they walked into the house. Frieda told her everything, giving her a hug before breaking the news of Gustav's condition.

"How didn't I see the poor man was starving? When have I become so blind?"

"Lily, you can't save the world. You do more than most. As I just told Frieda, you ladies have to give yourself credit for the good works you do."

Frieda saw the boy, standing staring into the fire, so caught up in his own thoughts he didn't turn when they came into the room. He looked better now he wasn't covered in muck and wearing rags. But he was stick thin. He had a nasty bruise on his lower jaw and a small cut across his eyebrow.

"Jack?"

Jack turned at the sound of his name, a look of terror on his face. "Alice? Is she with you?"

"Jack, Alice is fine. You did a fabulous job of looking after her. She is in the hospital for observation. The doctors want to check out her old injuries. Her father, Gustav, is with her."

Jack came closer. "I have to see Alice. What if he sends her away again? It will break her."

Frieda spoke softly, "Jack, sit down before you

fall down. Gustav is a good man. He never gave up on Alice and certainly didn't agree to her being adopted. Has someone sent a telegram to your mother? She must be worried sick."

Jack stared at the floor, his shoulders sagging. "We got robbed. I lost the money Miss Lawlor gave us."

"I will send your mother and Miss Lawlor a telegram. Inspector Griffin will send one to the sheriff of Deadwood Creek, won't you Inspector?" Lily prompted.

Frieda hadn't noticed the kindly policeman sitting on a chair in the sitting room. His lips pursed together, as if he was angry.

Inspector Griffin fidgeted before he stood up. "It's a medal they should give you son for what you did for that little girl. I'm sorry your journey ended the way it did."

Jack looked up. "You didn't do nothing, Mister."

Lily and Frieda exchanged a look of relief. They both knew Inspector Griffin would take personal responsibility for the way the police had treated Jack. The boy's words should help.

Lily took control. "Jack, why don't you go to

bed now. Tomorrow, Frieda will take you to the hospital to see Alice."

"You mean, you won't send me home?"

"You aren't a prisoner, Jack. You can go home any time you like but you are also welcome to stay."

"I'd like to wait until I can see Alice is happy."

Lily put her arm around his shoulders. "I think she won't be happy until she sees you. After you see Alice, I'm dying to hear the full story of your travels. I never met anyone who rode the rails before."

CHAPTER 41

The next morning, Frieda took Jack to the hospital and watched the reunion with tears in her eyes. Alice held onto Jack as if she'd never let him go. Jack offered his hand to Gustav who sat in a chair beside Alice's bed. The man stood up and pulled Jack into an embrace leaving both of them struggling not to cry.

"I'm so happy. All my dreams came true." Alice beamed as she held Jack's hand in one hand and her father's in the other. "When we leave the hospital, you can come and stay with us at my father's home, Jack."

Frieda caught the look of panic in Gustav's eyes. She wanted to reassure him, but Maria and Conrad arrived, Maria carrying a small gift in her hands. When Alice opened it, she found a new set of clothes for Agatha and a matching dress for Alice.

"They're beautiful, thank you."

"You're welcome," Maria's voice wobbled.

Frieda took Maria and Conrad for a coffee leaving the two youngsters to tell Gustav of their adventure. While they sat in the hospital canteen, Frieda explained Gustav being in hospital. "The poor man went out on strike to help support the women and then used his savings to find Alice. He met some men who said they were Pinkerton Detectives. He gave them money and never heard from them again." Frieda glanced at Conrad. "He can't get a good job as he was out on strike."

Maria took Frieda's hand. "You look exhausted, Frieda. You need to rest. I'll speak to Sarah and see if there is anything the Union can do to help Gustav."

Conrad didn't say a word.

"Thanks Maria. We best get back. I don't want Alice or Gustav to get too tired, they need their strength to recover. Gustav will have to fight the authorities to prove the adoption happened without his consent. That's assuming the Ackermans filed papers."

"That sounds expensive. Why does everything come down to money?" Maria asked as they strolled back to the ward.

Alice and Jack were deep in conversation but Gustav was sitting in the chair, his eyes closed, his lips thinned as if in deep thought.

Conrad took a step closer to Gustav, "I've had an idea. I'd like you to come and live with me, Gustav. I have plenty of room in my apartment and the rent is favorable. We could share a room and give the second bedroom to Alice. What do you say?"

Gustav didn't attempt to hide the relief on his face.

"You mean it?" he whispered. "Why? We don't know each other."

Frieda struggled to swallow the lump in her throat. Glancing at Maria's glassy eyes, she knew her friend felt the same.

"Gustav, we worked together for years even if we never spoke. We Triangle people must stick together in hard times. I wouldn't be where I am today but for Mr. Rosen helping me. Please come and live with me. If it makes you feel better, I have a selfish motive. You can act as chaperone when

Maria finally accepts my invitation to dinner. Mam taught me how to cook."

Maria blushed crimson as she poked Conrad in the arm. He pulled her to his side, planting a kiss on her head.

"I'm the best cutter in the Triangle and the bosses know it."

Maria chimed in, "He's modest too."

Everyone smiled as Conrad pretended to push her away from him. He pulled her close again before he spoke. "I can't promise anything but I will try to get your old job back. If you want it."

"Want it? I never thought I'd say this but I miss that old building. But they will never take on a striker."

"They will or they will lose their best cutter."

Gustav's eyes widened. "You would do that for me?"

"You would do it for your friends. You went out on strike to support my Maria and her friends. Why can't I help now?"

Maria hugged him as Gustav wiped the tears from his eyes. "This hospital, the smells they make my eyes water."

Frieda put her arms around herself. Everyone was so happy and she was thrilled for them but she was lonely. Maria had Conrad, all she had was a textbook and a year of daunting study ahead of her. In her mind, she went over again Patrick's words in the cab home the night before. We are family. But she didn't want to be his sister or whatever he thought of her as. She wanted more.

EPILOGUE

CHRISTMAS 1910, CARMEL'S MISSION

Lily sat back from the table watching her friends and family all chatting away. They had demolished the Christmas feast Cook and her friends had prepared for them. The women of the Sanctuary were having their own feast and party later on.

"How does my wife feel? Another year older and wiser?" Charlie dropped a kiss on her head as he moved to stand beside her chair.

"Wiser? Lily? I don't think those two words belong in the same sentence, do they?" Father Nelson teased.

"Father Nelson, you took an oath of charity, didn't you?" Inspector Griffin patted his stomach.

"Lily Doherty, I swear every time I come to your parties, I go home about ten pounds heavier."

Lily laughed, genuinely pleased her friends were having fun. Alice was upstairs with the other children, reading yet another of Jack's letters to her friends. Before Jack had left, Charlie had driven Alice, Jack and Gustav out to the farmlands where they thought the man Piper was working. They'd found Wolf and after a wonderful reunion, Piper had relinquished the dog back to Jack's care. He'd said Wolf pined for the children from the day he'd left them on the train. Alice insisted Jack take Wolf home to his house as he'd have a better life than couped up in New York. It was safe since the Ackerman's had disappeared one evening, leaving a huge mortgage and massive bills behind.

Father Nelson had accompanied Gustav and Alice to the orphanage where Alice had a tearful reunion with Miss Baker. Gustav caused the Matron to cry too but for a different reason. He told her to retire immediately or he would have her charged for what had happened to Alice. Mrs. Twiddle was also dismissed. Miss Baker had taken over management of the orphanage and Alice promised to visit her once a month. Gustav agreed on the condition he come too.

Lily stood up clinking her glass to get their attention. "Why don't we adjourn to the sitting room. The chairs are more comfortable for my aging bones."

"If your bones are aging, Lily darling, I'd hate to think what mine are doing?" Mr. Prentice smiled at her, his eyes warm and tender.

Lily linked arms with Mr. Prentice, amazed how well her old benefactor looked. After being a widower for years, he had recently married an old friend. Sadie was a tonic, insisting he retire and turn over the day-to-day management of his hotel chain to his well-trained staff.

She glanced at Charlie. He wasn't at all sure about her latest project but in true Charlie fashion was supportive and prepared to back her one hundred percent.

She stood up waiting until all conversation stopped.

"We are so grateful all of you came to our Christmas feast. As is our tradition, we have an announcement to make." She giggled as Kathleen's eyes flicked to Lily's stomach. That ship had sailed. She loved her children, but her family was complete. At least for now.

"Charlie and I have been talking about our next

project. As some of you know, I have become rather disillusioned over the last year."

"You and twenty thousand other women," Patrick joked falling silent as Frieda nudged him in the arm. "Sorry."

"Yes Patrick, I've been in good company. Those women and the men who supported them have given me a new idea. I or rather we want to open a factory."

"A factory?" Frieda echoed.

"Yes. I want to model our new factory on the Triangle factory."

"Lily, can you hear yourself? They can fire the girls for any reason. Those bosses lock their workers inside the factory. They don't let the girls talk or laugh never mind sing as they work. In fact, they deliberately place different nationalities next to one another not to teach everyone English but to make sure they can't chat. They charge the workers for their needles, their chairs, the thread they use. Sometimes, the electricity they use. Often the chairs have their backs removed to stop a worker from having a rest..." Frieda stopped as if she realized she was ranting.

She took a deep breath trying to ignore the look

of horror on her friends' faces. Didn't they know her at all?

"I don't mean how they treat their workers but some things they do, are nothing short of genius. For example, they brought the whole manufacturing process under one roof. We all have seen the sweatshops in the tenements where whole families worked on sewing buttons or making collars or cuffs or whatever it was. We've all seen the women or young children carrying loads of material on their backs or heads from one sweatshop to another. By bringing it all into one place, the Triangle owners have immediately cut costs and saved on waste."

"Since when did the bottom-line matter so much to you, Lily? Are you sure you are our Lily and not someone who just looks like her?" Father Nelson smiled but his eyes didn't light up as usual.

Lily ignored the stab of annoyance he would even think twice about her motives.

"As I was saying, they have made a lot of wise moves. For instance, they have taken out the middleman. At each stage of the process the sweatshop operator would add in his cut, he would make as much as possible on the deal usually meaning the workers lost out even more."

"Don't praise them Lily. They make profits off

the seat of their laborers whom they treat really badly."

"Yes Frieda, I know all that. I am not suggesting we copy all their changes. But we need to acknowledge the good ones. It makes sense to have the whole manufacturing process in one place. If we have a factory space big enough, we can do the same. We can buy the material in bulk to save on cost. We can employ the best cutters in the business. They will work for the same wages as they earn elsewhere, but we can entice them over to our factory by offering better working conditions. We can give them set hours not make them work as many as the boss wants or needs. An hour for lunch and a day that starts and finishes at set times."

"But Lily," Frieda interrupted.

"No, don't interrupt her. Let her continue, this could work." Mr. Prentice intervened. "But go back a little Lily. Explain to us how the process used to work and why you think the Triangle way is better. Because, although I am not in the shirtwaist business, even a grizzled old man like me has heard of Blanck and his friend and not for any good reason."

Charlie spoke up. "Lily in her excitement has rushed this a little. Let me explain. In the past, after the cutters had cut the pieces, the basters, typically young girls, would assemble the pieces together using long loose stitches. Then these pieces would move to the next sweatshop. We have all seen men, women and sometimes even children staggering under bundles of cloth. Their job was to take the assembled pieces to the next sweatshop where the machinists using pedal powered sewing machines would stitch them permanently together. Then they would go to the next stage and the next. At each stage, someone would be in charge and they would skim off their cut, reducing the amount paid to the people doing the work.

"So, you mean to cut this skimming by having all these jobs take place in one place?" Sadie clarified.

"Yes, but I want to do better. If we have electric sewing machines just like they do at the Triangle factory, we will speed up the process considerably. We can turn out more shirtwaists. Also, we won't lose time or risk pilfering by moving the product from one place to another."

Lily looked at each of her friends, they were listening to her now with a little less skepticism.

"Plus, if we move the sewing machine operators around on rotation, we get a skilled workforce. The girls, because they will be young women, will become better qualified plus it will keep the job more interesting. That may cut down on accidents. Do you know how many of the factory workers sew through their own fingers?"

"And then get charged for ruining the shirtwaists when they get blood on them!" Frieda added.

"We treat many of these injuries after the women finish their shifts. How some of them continue working is beyond me. They must be in agony." Patrick added.

"They don't have a choice, they can't afford to lose their job." Frieda smiled at Patrick as if to take the sting out of her remark.

"Our workers won't work in that state of fear. We will pay our workers a proper wage. At the moment they get paid by the piece. Some shirtwaist factory workers earn between two dollars, fifty cents and four dollars for working an eighty-four-hour week. In our factory, every person will have a quota to meet but it will be a fair one. Our sewing machine operators will earn five to seven dollars a week with an incentive scheme to earn more."

"Lily!" Kathleen looked at her as if she had two heads. Surely, she backed her plans.

"Stop saying Lily like that." Lily retorted. "The male cutters get twenty dollars. Which reminds me,

ORPHAN TRAIN STRIKE

I want to start a training program for female cutters. Who says cutters have to be men?"

Inspector Griffin coughed before he spoke. "I think I will need to give you police protection. You will upset many people with your new plans Lily."

Lily didn't care how many people she upset. The more the merrier if it made some of them sit up and have a look at their own factories.

"So be it. I also want a facility to mind these women's children. No more kids being left at home alone for hours on end. Our workers will bring their children to the factory. We will give them soup and bread. The older ones will go to school. Frieda and Patrick, I am counting on you to offer medical help."

Mr. Prentice exchanged a look with his wife. "But Lily, I hate to remind you, but your factory must make a profit."

Good grief, did he think she was stupid "Yes, I know that," she snapped. Charlie gave her a look perhaps his way of reminding her these people were her dear friends not the enemy. She softened her tone. "We can make a profit and treat the workers properly. We will attract the best workers and they will increase our profits. You wait and see."

"It's hard to say no when Lily gets this excited

about a project isn't it?" Inspector Griffin beamed his approval. She looked at him gratefully. It was nice when someone supported you regardless of how outrageous your plans seemed.

Mr. Prentice leaned in, telling her he was open to hear more. "Where do you want your factory? I know of several sky rises that have empty spaces."

"I don't want women working at those heights. I want to build a purpose-built factory. I aim to build it in Little Germany." This statement caused everyone to stare at her.

"Why there?" Frieda asked as Gustav opened his mouth to shut it again.

"I would like to try to re-build the community feeling in that area. You, Gustav and your other friends are testament to the good people living and working nearby."

Mr. Prentice opened his mouth, closed it again before finally saying, "Lily. Even for you that is going too far."

"Why? If we want to give these workers more comfortable conditions, we are best starting out with an empty space. It's better than trying to convert some old place isn't it?"

Mr. Prentice stroked his whiskers before asking, "So, put the emotional feeling aside and set the factory up down in Yonkers. I heard that's where Max Blanck is looking."

"It has to be in New York. There aren't enough skilled workers outside Manhattan." Lily hoped she sounded confident, she wanted to do this in New York. She hoped the plan for Little Germany would work but it would definitely be in New York. She had adopted the city as her home, and she didn't want to leave. But even she was prepared to admit it was an ambitious project.

"The price of real estate is an issue Lily," Mr. Prentice replied.

Lily sighed. Now she was glad she had discussed some of her plans with Anne Morgan. "Hopefully, not too much of an issue when you have friends whose family are in banking."

"By golly you have thought of everything. Does Morgan know he is funding a new factory?" Richard asked. "Never struck me as the type who would get too involved unless there was real money to be made. But then I don't know Morgan personally, only by reputation. Bankers don't have the best reputations in town."

"I don't know," Lily admitted. "Anne can deal with her family. Back to what I want for the workers. They are to have clothing lockers and we won't charge them for using them. They will have access to water. Did you know those Triangle owners charge their workers two cents a cup of water?"

"Why just girls? Don't the young men deserve a chance too?" Richard crossed his arms but the fact he was asking questions showed his interest. She knew Kathleen's husband had his own mission to change life for the poor of New York. He had introduced a scheme at his hospital where he charged the richer patients a little extra to help fund the costs of looking after patients who couldn't otherwise afford treatment.

"Yes, Richard they do. That's why our next project will involve the tailors. But for now, I want to build a model factory. I hope that by proving to the business community you can make money and treat workers like people, we will change their perspective. Maybe even bankers like Morgan?"

"That is something I would give my back teeth to see," Mr. Prentice said.

"Do you have plans for your factory? Even Anne will have to show the bank something," Sadie asked.

"I don't know if Anne will raise the money through the bank or through her friends. But yes, I have drawn up some simple plans. I'm no architect so forgive the simple lines."

She passed around the copy of the drawings she had made. She hesitated as she handed one to Gustav. He hadn't said anything up to now.

"Gustav, what do you think?"

Gustav glanced at the drawing. "Your plans worried me at first as I thought you meant to replicate the Triangle. But this looks different" His tone although respectable had a hard edge to it as if needed to be convinced.

"I am building a factory, but it will be the safest place I can make it. You have my word on that. I know you had some involvement when the fire inspectors visited the Triangle. I would like to hear your views on what safety measures I should take. I would also like some recommendations for the right people to call in as inspectors."

"Ja, I can do that. I will help. Conrad too."

Relieved, Lily smiled. She liked the Irish lad, Conrad and his girlfriend Maria. She'd invited the couple today but Maria wanted to spend it with her mother. Hardly surprising given it was close to the first anniversary of her father's death. At a cough from Charlie, she continued.

"See the factory will have large windows and

electric lights. We will use a window cleaner. I want natural light to flood the facilities. The workers will have proper toilets and washing facilities too. Who can keep white shirtwaists white if they have dirty hands?"

"Anything else?" Mr. Prentice asked drily.

"I expect our dear Lily will want you to put your hand in your pocket, dear." Sally said. "Lily, I'll help you with a small contribution from my personal funds."

Lily wanted to kiss Sadie for her support. "Thank you, Sadie."

Father Nelson coughed as if to cloak a laugh before he said, "Lily you are out to change the world."

"Nobody can do that, but I aim to change our community. It's time for us to take a stand. Carmel's mission was set up to achieve a certain purpose and to a point it worked but this is bigger. There is a greater need one that isn't fixed by sending children on Orphan Trains. I want, I need to do more."

She had a feeling, something she couldn't explain to anyone, not to Kathleen not even to Charlie. She had nightmares as bad as those she had suffered when she first became a working girl. They had started when she read about the Underwear factory fire in New Jersey in which twenty six people died. That building had only been four floors above ground not like the monsters they were building downtown.

She dreamed she was one of the girls in the fire, she was screaming, becoming trapped, not able to breath. She couldn't reach her children in some dreams, her friends in the other. The dreams terrified her. An all-consuming urge to work faster and open the new factories as soon as possible took over. But would she be fast enough?